Empire in the Sand

a novel

by
Shane Joseph

D1677369

Empire in the Sand
Copyright © 2022 Shane Joseph
All rights reserved
Published by Blue Denim Press Inc.
First Edition
ISBN 978-1-927882-70-2

Cover Design by Shane Joseph
Cover photography by Ken Solilo
Edited by Marie-Lynn Hammond

Library and Archives Canada Cataloguing in Publication

Title: Empire in the sand : a novel / by Shane Joseph.
Names: Joseph, Shane, 1955- author.
Identifiers: Canadiana (print) 20220265062 | Canadiana (ebook)
20220265119 | ISBN 9781927882702
    (softcover) | ISBN 9781927882719 (Kindle) | ISBN
9781927882726 (EPUB)
Classification: LCC PS8619.O846 E47 2022 | DDC C813/.6—
dc23

Look back over the past, with its changing empires

that rose and fell,

and you can foresee the future, too.

—Marcus Aurelius

Other works by Shane Joseph

<u>Novels</u>

Redemption in Paradise
After the Flood
The Ulysses Man
In the Shadow of the Conquistador
Milltown
Circles in the Spiral

<u>Short Story Collections</u>

Fringe Dwellers
Paradise Revisited
Crossing Limbo

Chapter 1

The old man crested the hill and looked down at the mainland ferry as it drew into Nanaimo harbour. He paused for breath. "This is a good time to be alive—or to die," he said to himself.

He sucked in the crisp air. It was a balmy ten degrees Celsius and he hoped spring would come early this year so that he could complete his work. At eighty-five, he didn't take life for granted anymore. A flock of snow geese swooped by overhead, heading downhill, their black-tipped wings drawing them languidly over the treetops. The weather was so warm these days, some birds didn't bother to fly south anymore. As he continued homewards, the smell of pine smoke wafted from his cabin, welcoming and enveloping him in the comfort and anonymity he had shrouded himself in these last ten years.

The cabin had been enlarged over time. Originally, he had wanted more space outside for his bees, and the A-frame log structure had only comprised a small living room with a fireplace, kitchenette, bedroom, toilet, and shower. The extension he put in five years ago held an office, and the satellite dish mounted on an adjacent metal tower gave him contact with the outside world via the internet. And the bees had found more space too as he had cleared the woods around the property and increased their population. Now they were busy keeping warm despite the mild winter by metabolizing their honey as they buzzed inside a row of white boxes lining the fence.

He entered through the back door, took off his coat, and hung it on a peg. He was neat; his living quarters were always tidy, testament to his Lutheran upbringing. He got upset with himself if he placed his reading glasses in the wrong place, or if the butter container wasn't closed, and these days he was starting to forget things. He missed Bruno, whose grave marked the southern entrance. He and his beloved dog had taken many walks through these woods over the years, and now he walked alone. But there had been no time for a new dog since Bruno got diabetes and was put down. There was no time.

The coffee was simmering. He had put it in the percolator before going out for his daily walk, a walk that took him downhill into the nearby crossroad hamlet for the newspaper, bread and milk, and a "good morning" chat with the general-store owner and his wife, the only souls he struck up a conversation with around these parts. His fear of talking to strangers since coming out west had become an ingrained habit. And yet, the daily walk had become one of the many rituals he practised to keep memory lapses from getting in the way.

He buttered his toast and took it on a plate with his coffee into his office. His desk faced large French doors from which he could see the bees in the garden and the Georgia Strait over the trees. This cabin was his refuge, but he had sudden misgivings. Should he be putting himself at risk at this stage of his life? Many people would give an arm and leg to be like him in this perfect place. Just sit back, enjoy the walks, the solitude, nature, his bees, until memory faded to the point where the next stop was a nursing home, or death. There weren't many more years ahead for him. Why screw up these last ones now? And yet he was not complete, and a restlessness dogged him. His whole life had been one of making wrong decisions. First, during the war, then at his work out east. He hadn't done much for mankind. In his misguided intention to do good, he had done bad. He looked fondly upon the bees. The bees were the only good thing in his life. His papa, if he were alive, would feel vindicated to see the bees flourishing after the family honey business had been decimated in Berlin. The bees, and his research, now gave him the impetus to keep going.

He switched on his computer and searched certain bookmarked websites for updates as he munched on his toast, taking occasional sips of coffee. Sand Pharmaceuticals in Toronto would be appointing a new president soon: Norman Samuels had announced his retirement.

Analysts were claiming this year, 2010, as a rebound year for the stock market after the meltdown in 2008, but the prospects for 2011 were uncertain. Then he checked his email. Sally Gordon had finally died yesterday, her nephew's recent email stated. He was glad she was gone; her last couple of months had been spent in a palliative haze. He sighed with satisfaction rather than sadness at this news. Eighteen out of twenty dead was a good trend line. How much more proof did they need? He felt he had earned the right to take the next step. There was no time.

He resumed the letter he had started and stopped writing many times, a letter he knew had to be written so that his soul could be at peace. The toast and coffee lay forgotten beside him.

Chapter 2

Avery Mann looked up at the giant tower extending into the sky. Cranes were adding new floors at the top, and scaffolding covered one side. To aid the construction, the ground floor facade that gave the building its period character had been removed and placed on the street to block one lane of traffic, impudently, he thought. But then the whole city was in a building frenzy and developers were kings; pedestrians and road traffic had to work their way around the ensuing chaos. He had been on one of those floors, enjoying a window seat that looked out over the Toronto Islands, the pinnacle of his achievements in those days, not so long ago.

He hated having to come in today, five years after the severance, but there were papers to sign, the final release from all claims on the company. Besides, a certain perversity compelled him to check out the old firm that had claimed his best years and spat him out like a sucked-out olive, even when there *was* gas left in his tank, as he had believed. *There IS still gas!*

The security guards were new, young, and zealous; they photographed him and issued him with a temporary visitor's permit—security in the city was tight these days, especially with the constant threat of terrorism. The visitor's badge that they hung around his neck on a red lanyard made him self-conscious. In the old days, his badge had never left his wallet, was never asked for; a nod at old Carlos or Tom in Security had got him through.

When he got into the elevator, there were a lot of youngsters around him, staring at or typing on cell phones, juggling lattes; no one spoke, except the guy who was carrying on a conversation with himself in a heavy Indian accent, assisted by a Bluetooth device to alert everyone that he had not flipped. Avery got off on the fifteenth floor, then realized that he was not in HR anymore. "They've moved up to twenty," a passing employee answered his puzzled enquiry. Avery took the remaining five floors by stairway and was glad that he was only slightly winded when he arrived at Human Resources. *I've got plenty of gas!*

There was no receptionist—probably downsized too. Closed glass doors faced him. "Use the phone and dial your party," said a sign beside a house phone. "Dial 0 for the company directory," it added.

He found Mark Preston's extension, but got only voice mail. *Now what the heck do I do?* He looked at his watch. He was ten minutes early and Mark was usually late for his appointments, which were normally double and triple booked; surprising that he had survived the cuts. But Mark was corporately fluid, seldom offering an opinion unless asked, always circumspect, always doing more with less, toeing the company line of whichever regime came into power through acquisition or downsizing—an employer's dream hire, especially in the C-suite.

Avery paced the vestibule between the elevator bank and the glass doors until an employee came out of an elevator and pressed a keypad in the wall to enter the inner sanctum.

"Can I come in too?" Avery held up his visitor badge. "I've an appointment with Mark Preston."

The employee, a man in his late twenties with brush-cut hair and shaved sides, frowned and said, "Mark was my boss. He left the company last week."

"But..."

"It was kinda sudden."

"Then he hasn't changed his voice mail. Who's his replacement?"

"They haven't posted the job yet."

"I've travelled a long way to get here. I need to sign some severance papers."

"Oh, you'd better see Olga then."

"Olga Beckmeyer? She still here? The hatchet lady! Sorry, that's an old joke."

The employee looked nonplussed at Avery's politically incorrect statement. He quickly badged them both in and hurried off to his cubicle with a "She's in the last cube down this corridor."

"I remember. She hasn't moved her spot, although she's moved five floors up."

Avery sauntered past the shoulder-high, beige cubicles, most of them now empty, until he got to the end, from where a loud voice emanated. The grey-haired woman was a shrunken version of the overweight matron who had once ruled the hallways, noted for her role as the person who escorted departing employees with their storage box of souvenirs amassed during employment—hence her unofficial title. During the eighties her cube had looked like it was on fire, for Olga had been a chain-smoker.

She finished her phone call and flushed when she saw Avery standing on the threshold of her untidy workspace. Her angular features had melted into a softer mass over the years. She cleared a folder off a chair, spilling papers on the floor. "Here, sit down. I've got your file, somewhere." No other greeting, just business as usual, head buried in paperwork again, avoiding the embarrassment.

"You haven't changed," Avery said, perching on the edge of the chair. "I'm surprised you're still here." He remembered how they used to joke about Olga's misshapen bust after she had a mastectomy and refused to do anything to hide the fact—yeah, the guys had been bad, misogynistic, they now called it. He wondered if that was why she was never promoted past the reliable "Manager, Human Resources," a position she had been in since he had joined the company. Now, the woman's whole chest was flat, but symmetrical.

She leaned back in her chair and sighed, as if tired of being busy. "They tried. But I knew too much. Everyone's dirty little secrets."

"But everyone's gone now. Well, almost. Is Brock slated to be fired yet?"

"Oh, no. He stays. He always stays. The little shit is tipped to be president when Norman retires. I've dirt on Brock too."

Olga had been one of long-standing president Norman Samuels's favourites. There had been rumours that she was his lover before she lost her breast.

"Brock was the architect of the downsizing that got me," Avery said.

"I remember. One of many downsizings. And yet, you were one of the better ones. I had to deliver the severance letters, listen to the stories of broken marriages that followed some of the high-spenders who had no Plan B. Go to Gory's funeral when he jumped off the building, hold his widow's hand, pat their little kids on the head. But it's all in the past. I'm retiring next week. Retiring!" There was a triumphant smile on her face now, as if to flaunt her achievement over all these poor sucks who could not make it to that stage where, instead of being walked out with your storage box of trinkets, you received a farewell party on the company's premises, at the company's expense, and where your stock options did not get wiped out before they vested.

"I came to see Mark. Heard he's gone."

She lowered her voice to a whisper. "Brock is outsourcing HR to a third party. Mark and I worked on the transition plan together. None of the staff here know yet."

"Trust you'll be out of here before that plan is announced?"

"My retirement was baked into the plan."

"I'm supposed to sign papers to make my departure official."

She moved some more files onto the floor and pulled out a thick green manila folder. "Here they are. Just sign the final release to say that we've paid you all your dues during your severance period. And it was a generous severance, if I might add. Nowadays, post 2008, employees get zip. Labour has suddenly gotten cheap. Sign here, then you can go. And I suggest you never return to this sorry place."

"Is any of the gang left on my old floor? Could I drop in on them?"

"You'll be disappointed. The floor is pretty empty. Brock's talking of moving to new digs in the 'burbs when the next round of cuts is over. Many work from home now. See these phones—they're dead hardware. Your phone number is portable, so is your LAN ID and your computer files. You rent a desk from an online app if you have to come in. Then you log in phone and laptop when you arrive and fire away. No pictures of the wife and kids, no trophies, no mementos—that's excess weight for the storage box when I escort you out for the last time. Mine is the only cube with a fixed address. That too was part of my deal with Brock."

"Why did you stay so long?"

She did something that surprised him. She placed her hands on her flattened chest. "Where could I go? First the right one, then the left. Then your husband leaves you because you're damaged goods. This life is all about appearances, and once you hit the point where parts start wearing down, you have no market value. Only other people's dirty little secrets keep you alive."

Avery rose. She was telling him things he knew and yet did not like hearing. "I guess I'll say goodbye, Olga. I wish you a good retirement."

"Have you had a good one up to now?"

"No. I'm still dealing with the loss, though it's been five years. A lot of shit happened in the meantime. But I will get over it. Coming here today has helped—it appears that I haven't missed much."

"I heard about Pat. Sorry. I will miss this place, though. Especially this cube, horrible though it is."

"Goodbye, Olga."

There were tears in her eyes for the first time.

On his way out, he saw the young employee who had let him in talking animatedly on the phone. The man waved goodbye to him and continued his phone conversation.

"Don't work so hard," Avery said under his breath. "You're being outsourced."

We were all outsourced. Eventually.

***

On his way down, on impulse, Avery got off on the fourteenth floor (it was actually the thirteenth, but people had been superstitious), his old floor in Marketing. Same glass doors barring entry, same house phone routine, voice mail from the few people he knew, until he got Barbara.

"Avery! So nice to hear your voice!" He had hired Barbara Spencer when she was fresh out of MBA school some twenty years ago.

"I'm by the elevators outside your department, and it's coming on lunch time. Can you scoot off for a quick bite?"

"No one to stop me. Hang on, I'll be out in a second."

She was dressed in a well-cut blue pantsuit, her formerly slim frame slightly broadened; with blond hair cut short and her thick-lensed glasses, she was still attractive, a good fit for a marketing department, for making presentations to focus groups, for dealing with ad agencies and media companies, for facing the press. She gave him a warm hug, then held him at arm's length. "I'm so glad you didn't vanish into the ether like everyone else. It's got kinda lonely around here."

"You must be a director at least by now, or else they would have sent you packing, like the rest of us."

"Correct. Director, Consumer Relations. Lots of letter writing, press releases, and that sort of thing."

"I was reading the articles emerging in the press about the cancer cases being pointed towards Sand."

She quickly looked about her and placed a finger to her lips. "Let's go out. Let me grab my coat."

When they exited the building, and he tried to cross the street to the Sand marketing gang's favourite watering hole, Mick's Irish Pubarette, she took his arm and steered him down two more blocks. They stepped over dirty snow hugging the sidewalks before entering a crowded Chinese restaurant, where they had to eat standing at a counter looking out at traffic.

"This way, I get to see who's around me, and who's coming or going," she explained, tucking into her hot and sour soup. Avery settled for a couple of egg rolls.

They caught up on their lives. She was separated now, with two kids in university. At closer quarters he saw the grey streaks in her hair mixed with the blond, and whenever she dropped her sunny demeanor there were lines around her hazel eyes.

She pushed her empty bowl aside. "Single life gives you a different perspective, doesn't it? I'm sorry about Pat."

"I didn't expect Brock to fire me at the time, the first time Pat came down with it in 2006, but I must have been moving around like the walking wounded."

"You were distracted. You needed time."

"Time is money in business. Anyway, being home after the severance helped me get her through her recovery that first time. But then the cancer came back with a vengeance three years later, and this time there was no stopping it."

"I'm really sorry."

He tried to change the subject, but only managed to step sideways. "So, what's with the cancers linked to Sand?"

"Nothing can be proven, of course. The five cases mentioned in the press were all taking our anti-allergy medication, Depo-Med, over a very long time and had switched to the generic version, Depo-Gen, when that came along, but they were also taking other medications from other pharmaceutical companies. There is no definitive link. I've had a lot of press releases to write recently."

"Positioning statements?"

She smiled, and the tiredness showed as she burped quietly. "You taught me well."

"Depo-Med—that was a drug I launched when I was head of your group. It became a cash cow in no time."

"Still is. That's why Martin...er, Brock is pulling out all the stops to head this debacle off. Rumour has it that he's readying the company for sale as soon as Norman's out of the picture."

"He's a good strategist. First, he outsources, then he sells. What will he be left selling? A bunch of patents?"

"It's tough to be a small player anymore, Avery. Big Pharma is just that, a game for big players."

"Have you had time to yourself since you and Bill split?"

"No. It's been six months, and I haven't stopped to think. I'm afraid if I do, the wheels will fall off. So, I keep going. This Depo-Med crisis has been good for me."

He placed his hand on her sleeve. "Listen, Barb. Don't con yourself. You said I needed time to heal? You need it too. Sooner or later the loss will get you. Start letting go of the grieving. Small doses to start."

Tears gushed into her eyes and she took deep breaths until the wave of emotion passed. "How do I do that and not end up like you? And I've got two kids to support."

"Call me sometime. I can be a sounding board." What was he saying? This woman was twenty years his junior. He who was looking to cut off all contact with people, inviting human drama into his life again? Didn't he have enough of it already?

"You sure?" The gratitude in her voice was thick. "I've talked to my sister. But she's an evangelical who doesn't believe in divorce. Wants me to get back with Bill, even if it means putting up with his new boyfriend."

"You can call on me. I don't keep too many friends either."

"But you were my first boss. How can I treat you as my confidante, especially on matters of the heart?" She looked at him, then looked away, raising her hands. "Besides, we're both single. Lonely, single people do stupid things when thrown together, don't they?"

"When you've run out of excuses, remember that I'm no longer your boss." He let the words sink in. He laid his hand in hers. After a while she squeezed it. Then she gave him a peck on the cheek.

"Thanks! You were also a good boss."

They hugged each other on the street corner before she vanished into the Sand building, promising to stay in touch. He gazed longingly after her, the kiss on his cheek tingling with invitation. He wished she would consider him more than just a good boss.

***

He took the subway back to his house in the suburbs. Watching his reflection in the train's window as it hurtled through the tunnels under the city, he realized that he was losing it. Here he was, at age sixty-five, when people of a previous generation had looked forward to kicking back, taking their pensions, and going to Florida to drink, play golf, and drown in the sun. Here he was, a widower, his pension blown, a family in turmoil, looking forward to living on the dregs of that company pension, and his pittance of a CPP and OAS. He *had* to make one more splash, do one memorable thing that the world would remember him by when everything he had done to date was now irrelevant and forgotten. What could that be, at his age?

He had given his best years, thirty, to Sand Pharmaceuticals. Seen it rise from a start-up with one patent to the mid-sized company it was today, employing six hundred staff, and with over a dozen patented drugs of commercial value. But now Brock was dismantling what they had built, blaming it on the competition. Avery remembered his father's words the day they had been down at the quarry breaking stones to build the old cottage: "You must haf a place to hide from the world. The world is cruel. See vat they did to us in Germany. I was saving lives, driving an ambulance during the blitzkrieg, but because your mother was Jewish, they put us in the camps."

He had built his own refuge too after selling his father's cottage. Avery had moved further inland into swamp country, thick with mosquitoes and thin of people, on the shore of a shallow lake rich in trout. He had built his cottage in a clearing above the water line with plenty of sunlight and used solar panels for off-grid electricity, a well for water, and septic for sewage. It had a wood stove and a fireplace, and he could retreat into it for months at a time. The acreage around him was populated with deer, and he could kill one, with a permit, to last him a whole winter. The nearest store was ten kilometres away, the nearest neighbour a kilometre, unless you counted the solitary log cabin on the other side of the lake, only visible through binoculars.

Today's visit had ended all ties that held him to the city. Was it now time to retreat to the cottage and live out his last days? Or become a snowbird and live a half-life chasing the sun in Florida? Tempting prospects both, and yet something bothered him: that missing last hooray, whatever it was. It had to be a hooray with a win attached to it, not a mere ceremonial signing of papers like what had taken place with Olga today.

As he alighted at Kennedy Station, the weather on this frigid February day had turned blustery, sending needles of cold down his throat and down through to his bones. He stifled a cough, and it struck him as ironic that Pat too had once taken Depo-Med for her asthma. He had actually recommended it to her, and she had discussed it with her doctor, who had subsequently prescribed it.

He turned up his collar and walked the five blocks north, head bent against the wind, thinking.

Chapter 3

Avery warmed a can of soup while checking his voice mail. Damian had left a message in his typical cryptic style: "Dad—call me, something's come up."

Since his son's call three years ago, when Pat was undergoing chemo after her cancer had resurged, Avery was wary of responding to Damian's "something's come up" calls. On that occasion, it had been a red-hot tip on an investment fund. Preoccupied with Pat's deteriorating condition, and due to Damian's insistence that he needed to improve his retirement nest egg, Avery had let his son deal with that financial transaction by signing his trading powers over. It was only after the funeral several months later, in January 2009, that Avery lifted his head to find out that due to the stock market meltdown the previous fall, his hot new investment fund had tanked. Damian merely shrugged and said that they would "make it back." They still hadn't, despite the rebound in stocks last year. Avery's other investments were just beginning to limp back, and he couldn't pull anything out without converting paper losses into real ones. He realized that he couldn't afford to retire at the usual retirement age of sixty-five anymore, when his severance package ran out. He would have to look for another job soon. Even the government was now talking about scrapping mandatory retirement. *Fine for them, but now we poor suckers have to work until we die!*

He drew back the blinds in his living room and saw a string of cars parked opposite Stan Barclay's house. There had been a lot of activity at Stan's recently as the man was gearing up for his three-peat attempt to run as Centrist candidate for the riding in the imminent federal election. Avery had avoided Stan in recent weeks, because he knew he would be asked to assist again. Stan had run unsuccessfully against Tory Bernard Phelps in

2004 and 2006, and Avery had helped him in the second election by volunteering at Stan's campaign office, fielding calls, and distributing lawn signs. Avery had helped partly because he wanted to take revenge on his former employer for unceremoniously dumping him that same year—Dr. Phelps had been a board member at Sand before resigning to pursue a career in politics. But this time, Avery wanted to steer clear of politics, steer clear of the human race if he could, hence the focus on his cottage in the boonies.

The phone rang. Stan's Jamaican accent, prominent despite having lived many years in Canada, flowed down the line. "Avery, how you doin,' man? Saw you com home. We having a small meeting here. Wanna com over? The missus having some roti and ginger beer going. I gotta small job for you."

Stan's infectious enthusiasm was inescapable, and Avery wondered whether it was a clever pretence to cover a deeper depression that had started to emerge in recent years. After a string of upwardly mobile moves, Stan's trajectory had plateaued. Being neighbours for over twenty years, Avery had seen this immigrant family make it to the big time in incremental steps. First, it had been the solitary jerk chicken restaurant at the corner, funded by life savings and a bank loan; then a few more outlets in Scarborough, and after Stan's two sons came out of university, a chain across the GTA—a great business success for a poor immigrant who had come to Canada thirty years ago with only a suitcase of clothes. A hard working, upright family that went to the Anglican Church on Sundays and gave generously to charity. During the winters, as Avery had not graduated beyond using a puny shovel, Stan always offered to clean Avery's driveway after every snowstorm using his huge snow blower.

Now, Avery found it difficult to refuse his old friend. "Okay, I'll come over in a bit. Keep the curry warm."

He finished reading his newspaper, ate his soup, cleaned up, and walked over. Some of the parked cars had driven away. The Barclay house, once a standard suburban three-bedroom bungalow like his own, had been extended with every wave of Stan's growing business empire. A second floor, a garage, and a pool in the backyard had been added over the years.

Stan, dressed in casual sweatpants and a tee-shirt, opened the door and beamed. A bearded bear of a man with an infectious smile, Stan had made his reputation by standing at the entrance to his restaurant, greeting everyone with a handshake or a hug, and offering them samples of jerk chicken while they stood in line to order take-out. Today, he gave Avery a hug that smelled of a strong deodorant, sweat, and spice. "Avery, man! Good to see you. Com in, com in."

The usual suspects were hanging around the dining room table amidst plates of left-over food and half-drunk glasses of ginger beer: Doug Saunders, a retired school teacher and Stan's campaign secretary; Asif Mikani, a local businessman who ran a string of ethnic food distribution outlets in the city and who had started out at the same time as Stan (he supplied the raw materials for Stan's restaurants); and an older white man of about seventy whom Avery did not recognize.

Lizzy Barclay came out of the kitchen with a steaming plate of rice and curry. "Ah—why you late? Sit, sit. I kept this hot for you and forbade these men from having another morsel until you ate."

Lizzy was lighter skinned than her husband, stout, and matronly, with a generous heart. She had visited Pat often with chicken soup during those last days.

"Thank you, but I've eaten." Avery said.

"Then I gonna put it in a bag for you to take home for your dinner," she replied, unflappably. She left the plate beside him and went into the kitchen, returning with a bottle of ginger beer and a plastic container. "Here, maybe you will drink this, at least." She flipped the top open with a bottle opener. "This be a long meeting today, has been going on all mornin'." She emptied the rice into the plastic container and wagged a finger at him, "Now, you take this home and eat it come dinner time. I tol'

Pat I was gonna keep an eye on you, though you been avoiding us." With a wink, she returned to the kitchen.

"Let me introduce you to John Dodds," Stan waved over to the older man, who rose and shook Avery's hand with a bony but firm grasp. Avery marvelled at how Stan could flip out of his patois and resume a formal colonial British accent the moment he got down to business.

"John chairs the local Sixty-Five Plus Club that has a membership of over four hundred. They are also networked with other seniors clubs in the GTA. This is a group we have not focused on in past campaigns." Stan had an eyebrow cocked at Avery.

After the usual opening round of jokes between the men, Stan brought Avery up to speed. "We are going to run our campaign with two prime thrusts this time, concentrating on constituents we ignored the last time—youth and seniors."

"How do you know the other guys aren't doing the same?" Avery asked. He was skeptical about local efforts because national advertising trumped everything. If people wanted a right-wing prime minister, they were going to vote for their local riding's right-wing candidate whether they knew him, liked him, or not. Avery had voiced this belief several times to Stan in the past but hadn't been able to convince his friend.

John Dodds spoke for the first time. His voice was reedy, but there was a steely determination in it. "They can't go after the seniors after what they've taken away from us over the last five years: frozen pensions, clawed back old-age security, cuts to health care, the list is endless."

"And my sons, who have university degrees, have no jobs," Asif said in his accented English. "I have to employ them in the family business. What happens if we had no family business? We came to this country to give the young people a chance—they are now worse off than us."

"Same here," Stan said. "Rohan and Dwayne have MBAs, but Bay Street didn't want them."

"Thank God!" Lizzy piped up from the kitchen. "You gonna work all your life? De boys have taken over de restaurants and expanded them, and allowed you to play at your politics. You better make sure you win this time."

"Pressure, pressure." Stan grinned and poured more ginger beer.

Avery didn't want to disagree with the men at the table. But his own son Damian had done all right, and on Bay Street too. If one judged success by a paycheque, that is. As if pre-empting his thoughts, Stan said, "I know you have not had the same experience as we've had, Avery. Damian is a big guy on the Street, and we are happy for him, but he is one among the lucky minority."

"But I tell you,"—Lizzy had come out of the kitchen and was looking at them with hands on her hips—"dat boy of yours, Avery—he too greedy. I used to give him beans when he was growing up in the neighborhood and showing off all de time. Always wanting to parade his latest bike or his latest Walkman that you bought him. And later, with dat sports car. Pat was worried about him until she went to her grave."

"Lizzy, Lizzy—we not here to talk about de children. I got a political campaign to run, girl." Stan was starting to look annoyed and slipping back into his patois.

"Okay, I be going now to de women's auxiliary meeting. But I hope you men will also campaign to bring back liberal values that we so proud of. Values that gave us immigrants a chance to succeed. I hope it is not only politics and winning that matters."

After Lizzy had gone upstairs to shower and dress for her outing, the men sipped their drinks, sobered by her outburst.

"Sorry about that, Avery," Stan said after a while. "Lizzy means well."

"No offence. She speaks from the heart. That's what makes her a good friend. I'm so grateful she was there for Pat."

Doug Saunders cleared his throat and looked down at his notes. "Gentlemen, can we get down to this meeting, please? Time is moving on. The writ is expected to drop at the end of March, six weeks from now, and we need to get our ducks in order."

"Yes," Stan said, his voice resuming its businesslike tone. "As I said—youth and seniors. It's not only about the immigrant vote anymore. Dwayne's and Asif's boys have taken care of the youth sector. They have put together a social media campaign that has kicked off. I know nothing about this stuff, but now I have a Twitter handle and a Facebook page and I am supposedly twittering and getting lots of 'likes,' whatever that means. That's supposed to connect with the youth, they tell me. They bought me the latest iPhone which I am supposed to check four times a day." There was no sign of the phone anywhere, so Stan was probably still going through this technological change.

"What do you want me to do for you?" Avery asked. He had not returned Damian's voice message and was now anxious to get back home.

Stan's eyes narrowed. "I want you to work with John here. Many seniors don't vote because they can't get out to the polling stations, especially if the weather is not good. Now this election will be in May sometime so it should not be too bad, but you can never tell with our crazy seasons anymore. We are thinking of organizing a convoy of vehicles to escort seniors from their homes to the polling stations. I wanted you to work with John on that."

"Okay—sounds like a plan," Avery said, and nodded at Dodds. "I'll get in touch with you later this week and we can work out the details." Turning back to Stan, he asked, "How close are we this time?"

"Pretty close, according to our polls. A couple of hundred votes could mean the difference between Phelps and me."

"The gap has narrowed."

"Broken promises over two campaigns will do that." Stan rose, and this time there was a tremor in his voice. "I gotta do it this time, Avery. Three strikes and you are out—not only in baseball. Can I count on you?"

Avery picked up his plastic container. "Yes, you can. Thank Lizzy for the food. Good day, gentlemen!"

Stan saw him to the door. On the threshold, the big man shook his hand and held it. "You not getting out much dese days, Avery?"

"The house is kinda empty. I walk the malls in the winter, and the parks in the summer."

Stan lowered his voice to a whisper. "You should try that online dating thing. Our Doug's been at it since his divorce two years ago. He says he has a new date every week. Every week, man!"

"He must be pretty 'dated' if none of them are sticking around."

"He says he don't want dem sticking 'round. He's protecting his financial assets."

Avery started down the steps. "Maybe I'll give it a whirl sometime. Beats watching TV."

***

As he crossed the street to his house, Avery realized how down-home and ad hoc Stan's campaign was compared to the well-oiled one he could imagine being run out of Phelps's headquarters in the Bluffs area. And Phelps's team of supporters would also be different: WASP, grey-haired, business elites, and landowners, with an army of university students to telemarket and run social media campaigns to a scripted strategy. But Stan had the immigrant underbelly of this riding, the hopeful hordes, who, like Avery's father three generations ago, had come to this country and built it to what it was, and who were now angrily watching it slip away to a nineteenth century model where wealth was again concentrating in the hands of a secretive and protectionist minority. Add disenfranchised seniors and underemployed youth, and Stan might just make it this time. A couple of hundred votes could be the decider, Stan had said. Perhaps this campaign was worth fighting, if it would make the difference.

***

"She wants a divorce." Damian's voice sounded cracked on the phone. "And so do I."

Avery gripped receiver tightly at his end. "Hang on now. I know you've had your differences, but you don't have to be so drastic."

"It's been going on for some time now. She's seeing other guys. I caught her laptop full of email from a dating site."

20

Avery swallowed. "But...you have a son. You have responsibilities."

"This is the twenty-first century, Dad. Marriage is anachronistic. I should never have married. It's been one big tie-down."

"So, what can I do, since you've already made this decision?"

"Can you take Paul out for a drive, to a movie or something? Syl and I have to sit down to do the listing our assets—it could get messy."

After the initial announcement of his intentions, Damian's voice had taken on a routine tone. It was as if he was discussing the agenda for a corporate meeting.

"I'll come over," was all Avery could say as the disappointment in him welled like bile. He replaced the receiver on its cradle and staggered into the kitchen to get a glass of water. Lizzy's food parcel was lying on the counter. Absentmindedly, he placed it in the fridge—Pat had never let food go to waste—poured himself a glass of water, drained its contents, refilled, and took it into the living room. Then he started shaking all over.

Damian, his only son, disappointing him again. Avery had given him everything, brought him up as a privileged kid, including providing him access to private schools, an MBA from Queens, a sports car, and a deposit on a condo Damian had purchased downtown fifteen years ago to be "close to the action on the Street." By now, Avery had even forgiven his son those impulsive investments in 2008 that had cost him his retirement, in the hope that it had taught Damian a valuable business lesson. But this divorce, after a ten-year marriage that had started to go downhill in its seventh year—the seven-year itch, or curse—was hard to stomach. And in a family whose patriarchs had stayed married through thick and thin until death did them part from their spouses. What hurt most was Damian's flippancy about it—as if he were trading in an old car!

He looked at Damian's and Sylvana's wedding photograph on his mantelpiece. Two bright stars who met in university and fell in love, and were going to change the world—Damian in finance on Bay Street, and Sylvana to expand her father's financial planning practice that she was to inherit. The couple in the picture: Damian with curly blond hair like his mother, pencil-line mustache that was the fashion then—also to give his weak features a sharpness—was dressed in a white Armani tuxedo and tie, eyes looking on the world as if to devour it; red-haired Sylvana in a crimson gown with a tiara of red roses in her hair, svelte and intelligent, but hiding an anger in those wide green eyes that could flare up if provoked, like her Neapolitan mother. There were other pictures of the family, after Paul came along less than nine months into the marriage, making Avery wonder whether there had been another motive for this union, and whether the crimson, high-waisted wedding dress had been chosen to hide the swelling of Sylvana's belly. Pat, who saw only the good in people, had shrugged it off, rationalizing it as: "Oh, if they knew they were going to be together, they must have let love rule the day."

He walked over to the mantelpiece and picked up the framed collage of Paul's pictures, one photograph for each year of the boy's life, stopping at year ten, the last one taken a month ago: the progress from an amorphous baby in a crib, to a toddler building blocks on the floor, to a kid on a tricycle, to one on a swing, to a withdrawn one holding an iPad. When Avery had questioned the iPad, Damian had said, "Aw, Dad, gimme a break—it's the tool of his generation. Like my Walkman or your cassette recorder. Besides, it shuts up all those dumb childish questions, the ones I used to ask you and interrupt you reading the newspaper. Now, Paul asks Google instead." Paul certainly was an informed kid, when he chose to talk, which was not often.

Avery forced himself to put on his overcoat and step out through the side door into the garage. He was not relishing what lay in store for the rest of the afternoon.

His eight-seater minivan was in superb condition, and this cheered him somewhat. He had bought it soon after Pat passed away, when the recession was biting and prices for vehicles had dropped. The old Cadillac, in mint condition, had reminded him too much of his former corporate life, and of Pat, memories he knew he had to move beyond if he was going to have another chapter in his life. The new vehicle had also helped him transport building materials out to the cottage that he had painstakingly built over the last two years. The all-season cottage would enable him to sell this house, the last reminder of his former life as a corporate executive, husband, father, and caregiver. He wondered whether the van was the reason Stan had earmarked him to run transport for the election. Stan knew how to peg his supporters. *Okay, Stan, I'll help you this last time. After that, I'm out of here.*

But could he really leave, he wondered, as he drove towards Forest Hill where his remaining family lived. *Can I ever escape from being a father?*

***

The house was a sprawling three-storey Georgian-style structure: the facade was brown brick with dormer windows standing like sentries overlooking the driveway. It was a utilities sinkhole, Avery had concluded, soon after the newly married couple had bought it, but Sylvana had got her father's contacts in the building industry to gut the inside, install new wiring, plumbing, a gas furnace, and an air conditioning system that regulated temperature via a computer, remotely, while the occupants were at work. The ultra modern kitchen had every appliance that Avery knew nothing about; all he knew was that various meals started cooking at different times of the day, triggered by signals send via smart phones, and the food was wonderfully piping hot and ready to be served to guests, or whenever his son and daughter-in-law arrived home, which was often at different times and rather late in the evening. A gardener was paid to maintain the lawn and the giant oak trees that ringed the house, and an imported housekeeper from South America kept everything humming indoors, including an eye on Paul who spent most of his time alone. Two SUVs sat in the driveway, which would mean that the vintage Jaguar Damian had bought recently, for summertime driving, must be in the garage.

Damian met him at the front door. His son looked a bit haggard, his hairline already starting to recede. He was dressed in baggy sweats, and led Avery into the spacious family room, which had blankets piled on the couch and clothes strewn on plush armchairs. A laptop glared blankly from a side table. Empty beer bottles perched on various parts of the remaining furniture, and a pizza box lay open on the coffee table with its half-eaten contents curling up in the dry air.

"Maria having a day off?"

"Maria quit." Damian sighed and sank into the blanketed couch. Avery observed that his son might have been sleeping here the night before, or for many nights already. "She couldn't take the shouting."

"Seems quiet to me now."

"See the barricade?"

Avery turned in the direction Damian was pointing, at the stairway to the upper floors. A gate, similar to the security fence they'd had when Paul was a baby, was mounted on the bottom step.

"Syl lives upstairs now. And I live. . .here. We have called a temporary truce to regain our strength before 'negotiations' resume."

"Where's Paul?"

"In his room."

"Upstairs? Am I allowed to cross the picket line?"

"I'll phone him." Damian picked up his cell phone and hit a speed dial number. "Grandpa is here."

After a while, a small figure crossed the landing and slid downstairs.

Avery went over to the barricade and looked at his grandson on the other side. Paul looked scared and withdrawn.

"Hi, buddy!"

"Hi." A weak reply, hushed, as if Paul was scared to wake someone in the vicinity.

"How about a ride up to the cottage?"

From behind him, Damian laughed hoarsely. "You've been promising that for a while. Today might be the perfect day."

Paul remained silent. Avery prodded, "What say you, Paul?"

Paul shrugged. "I dunno."

"Go get your coat."

"And some clothes, in case you have to stay overnight." Avery caught Damian's wink.

When Paul had retreated upstairs, Avery asked, "Is this negotiation going to take all night?"

"You never know. There is a lot of baggage to get through."

"But you've had comfortable middle-class lives. It was my generation with the baggage."

"We piled it on during our marriage. Behind every purchase was an argument. Behind every kid I didn't want to give her, including Paul, was an argument."

"Where is Sylvana right now?"

"Gone to her mother's to regroup. She'll be back at five. You'd better be gone by then."

"She hates me too?"

"She hates everything and everyone that reminds her of me. She hates Paul too at the moment. He's half of me, just as you are."

Watching his son hunched on the couch, hair tousled and a shadow of beard marring his boyish features, Avery wanted to reach out and comfort the little boy that he knew lurked inside, a little boy who had never quite grown up, because he, Avery, and Pat, had never let Damian grow up.

"I'm there if you need me."

"I know, Dad."

"Perhaps, this episode will give you some time to re-examine your life's choices. The big house and the fancy cars and Bay Street aren't everything, you know."

"I guess the big house is kind of fucked now, and maybe the cars too, although I'll retain the Jag. But Bay Street is all I have, and I'm never giving that up." Then, something suddenly occurred to him. He leapt from the couch and went to his laptop. "Gotta show you something."

He scrolled through to an email that Avery recognized was from the president of Damian's company, Premier Investments.

"What the heck—?"

"Yes—isn't it great, Dad? My first IPO. To be managed all on my own."

"Can you do it at this time? With all this domestic turbulence?"

"All the more reason to do it now. If this deal goes through, I'll make partner in the firm. Imagine the alimony then? No, I have to conclude this separation deal now, while Syl's income and mine are about equal and all I have to think about is child support." Damian had a desperate look on his face and he quickly closed his laptop when an upstairs door slammed. "Don't tell Paul any of this." His voice had dropped to a whisper.

Avery didn't like the look on Damian's face, like that of a trapped animal zigzagging to flee from being put inside a cage, the look of terror not to be relinquished until an escape route opened somewhere. He tried to hide his own emotions. The company mentioned in the IPO deal glared back at him: Sand Pharmaceuticals.

As if pre-empting his father's thoughts, Damian said, "I hope you don't have any hard feelings about your old company getting into the big time when you're no longer there to share in the spoils?"

"I went to the old firm to sign my final release today. The place has changed. You couldn't drag me back there with the proverbial barge pole."

"Good. Our president picked me because he thought I might have some insider knowledge on the players, like Martin Brock."

"I'm surprised Brock didn't recognize you and veto your nomination."

"You forget that Mann isn't my surname anymore."

"Oh, yes. I forgot. That's another hard one to get used to." Damian had decided to take his mother's last name, Morgan, when he went to MBA school, and later into the working world—it fit better with his social media image.

"Brock wasn't my friend."

"I know. I used to overhear conversations between you and Mom in the evenings. Especially that time you started drinking hard."

"I got over it. I got over him."

"Good. Then you could tell me more about what makes him tick. He's driving things from the Sand end." Damian's voice was getting animated; he got this way when he was chasing a new deal. He had been this way since childhood when getting ready for his next exam paper, which he'd planned to ace and usually did. But Avery's gaze was focused on the wiry figure descending the stairs with a knapsack on his back.

"Not now. Maybe later. Now I'm going to focus on your son and get him out of this pathetic place."

Chapter 4

The sun was going down when they left the city, an orange blur behind gathering clouds heavy with moisture. Avery turned to 680 News, but the weather forecast was not due yet. It would take them about three hours to get to their destination, and he hoped the precipitation would hold off. He chided himself for not checking the forecast before setting out. But the conversation with Damian had been unsettling.

"What weather do you want, Grandpa?" Paul perked up with sudden interest from the passenger seat.

"How about north of the Kawartha Lakes, and about twenty kilometres east of the provincial park."

Paul was already on his iPad, his fingers pulling maps apart, dragging, expanding, moving beyond.

"Snow," he said after a while. "Lots of snow."

"Thanks."

"Give me your address and I'll have my GPS point the way," Paul said.

"There is no address right now. How about fire code 160035, Kawartha Lakes?"

"No good," Paul said after a while. "Google doesn't recognize that."

"Then you'll have to trust in my good old instincts. What I was raised with."

Paul slumped back, disinterested. When Avery next glanced over, the boy was watching a movie on his iPad.

Avery stopped at a grocery store in Peterborough. The cottage was stocked with dry rations, but he wanted fresh food: bread, milk, eggs, and fruit to last them in case they were snowed in. This adventure would be good for Paul after all.

The snow came down east of Peterborough after they turned onto a county road. Within minutes they were in a snowscape: trees, road, road signs, all covered in thick white clumps that illuminated the darkness but left them in a lost world. Their pace reduced to a crawl as the heavy flakes kept hitting horizontally into the headlights. The road had completely vanished. Avery caught the tail lights of a truck ahead and hung onto them to find his way in case the van landed in a ditch by straying too close to the shoulder. He felt a tinge of fear surge through him. He had never been out to the cottage in this weather before; his previous trips had always been planned ahead with weather taken into consideration. Besides, he had his grandson with him, which deepened his sense of responsibility.

"You enjoying this?" he asked aloud, trying to sound nonchalant.

"Nah. It's boring. There's nothing to see."

"Isn't it dangerous? Aren't you scared?"

"Nah. We can always call 911 if you go off the road."

"Do you kids always feel so…so…secure? You're only ten."

"The movies I watch are scarier."

"That's the problem. In your world, the movie always ends and you get to put the lights out and snuggle up in bed. There's no bed here until we make it to the cottage."

What am I doing here — trying to scare a kid? But his smugness is getting to me. Being scared in this situation is normal. Go on kid, get scared!

"We can call Dad. I always call Dad or Mom when it gets too much." Paul fished out his cell phone. After fiddling with it for a while, his voice went into high pitch. "There's no signal." *Take their techno-crutches away and they become normal again.*

"Try mine." Avery slid his BlackBerry over.

"This is old-fashioned."

"Quit complaining and try dialling."

This time, he got through. "Dad? Grandpa and I are in a snowstorm."

Oh shit!

"You don't have to tell him that!" Avery snapped.

"Dad wants to know if you plan to turn back?"

"Tell him that there is no turning back on this road, we keep going till we reach our destination. Another thirty minutes or so and we should be there."

"He wants to talk to you."

"Tell him I don't have time. I need both hands on the wheel and my eyes on the road."

"I'll put him on speaker."

The next thing Avery knew, the phone was stuck in his face and Damian was yelling at the other end. "Where the fuck are you two?"

"Driving. Getting away from civilization."

"You gotta stop at a gas station or mall or something until the weather clears."

"Doesn't look like it's gonna clear. Besides there are no gas stations on this stretch. And the last mall was in Peterborough."

"Where the heck did you buy this cottage?"

"In God's country."

"You're putting my kid at risk."

"Yeah. And your divorce is not?" Turning to Paul, Avery yelled, "Now that you've had your chat, turn that bloody phone off. We'll talk to your father later."

He turned his eyes back on the road; the tail lights in front had disappeared. Now he had only the deep tire tracks in front to follow. The snow was pelting down harder and visibility was reduced to a few metres ahead. He slowed down to ten kilometres per hour.

"Dad wants me to keep the phone running until we arrive somewhere safe."

"Oh, give that to me. We'll lose battery and then we'll be really screwed." Avery grabbed the phone, switched it off and stuck it between his thighs.

Paul looked petrified. Defeated, he turned towards the front window. "What happens if we go in the ditch, Grandpa?" The boy's voice was quivering now.

"Then we stay in the ditch until help comes."

"Will your phone still work?"

"I've never hit blind spots on my previous drives. But then I don't use my phone much while driving. So, let's hope we don't have to find out the bad news today."

They came to a crossroad, and Avery recognized it as a landmark despite snow covering the road signs: the tall grain silo next to a windmill, both shrouded in snow but with their outlines visible. *Thank God for that nostalgic Dutch immigrant who decided to build himself a symbol of home!* "Okay, ten more minutes—make that twenty in these conditions—and we should be at the cottage."

The rest of the way was darker and gloomier, narrower with the increasing snowfall. What a difference bright sunshine made in this part of the world! Elk Lake emerged on their right and Avery followed the road that had turned into a trail until they came to the gate leading to the cottage. His property was the first one of only two on this last stretch of dirt road, the other being a kilometre away, before the wetlands took over. He left the van on the road and started unloading the provisions. "Come on—it'll be a five-minute walk from here. Bring all your gear and don't forget your mitts—it's freezing cold outside and the cottage takes a while to warm up."

∗∗∗

"You don't have internet?" Paul was fiddling with his iPad, looking incredulously at Avery as he stowed away the groceries. The cottage smelled of the new paint he had given it on his last visit, and the fireplace had been lit and was starting to crackle.

"Didn't think I needed it here. In fact, I come here to get away from the internet."

31

Paul flung himself on the old couch. "Oh heck. A whole evening wasted." He drew his knees together and shivered. He looked scared even though he was with his grandfather.

Avery pointed to the book rack lining the wall of the living room. "I'm sure you could find a book to interest you in that collection. All my books since childhood are in there, the selected ones only, the ones worth keeping."

"Books are boring. Do you have a TV?"

"Nope. I buy the newspaper whenever I go into town."

Avery could see that his casual retorts weren't doing the boy any favours. "A drink, perhaps?"

"Coke, please." The word "Coke" seemed to dispel some of Paul's unease even as he said it.

"Now, *that* I've got." Avery poured himself a scotch on the rocks and a Coke for Paul, fetched the drinks over, and sat beside the boy on the couch. There was enough wood inside to keep them warm through the night. The woodshed was a few steps from the cottage, but he wasn't about to go outside again because the snow was knee-deep already. Snowmelt dripped off their coats hanging by the door and joined the puddle left by their boots on the wooden floor.

"I'm sorry about what's happening to your mom and dad."

"Why do people divorce?"

"It's not happened to me, so I can't tell. I guess it's because they can't live together anymore. When they fight too much."

"But they've always fought."

"You know that your mom and dad will still be a part of your life, don't you? And you've got me."

"If you're going to live here, then I won't see you." Paul was looking accusingly at him, and Avery looked away.

"I'll come and visit. Besides you'll be so busy with school and stuff, you won't have time for an old man like me."

"My friend Tom says that when your parents divorce, you get to have two homes. And your mom always tries to give you better presents than your dad, because they're always showing off to you."

Avery sipped his drink quietly. He was running out of conciliatory words.

"I guess so."

"And your mom and dad get married to other people and have lots more kids, and they forget you."

"That's not true." Avery was wishing he now had the internet and cable TV and video games and a thousand other distractions. "I guess you've never talked about this to your dad or mom, have you?"

"No, they're so busy, when they're not fighting."

So, you bury yourself in an iPad.

"When I was sad at times, I used to get out and jog. I got skis and snowshoes in the back. Do you feel like going out and throwing some snowballs?"

"Nah."

"You city slickers will become obese by the time you get to my age if you don't exercise."

"That's what Dad tells Mom when he wants to make her mad."

Damian must definitely want this divorce.

Avery shrugged off his reluctance to go outdoors. "Come on. Tell you what—I'll rustle up some food, and then let's get those snowshoes on and take a walk back to the van at least. Get us some fresh air before we turn in for the night."

***

Later that night, as he stared into the simmering fireplace, Avery chuckled when he reflected on their recent walk in the snow. Despite the snowshoes, Paul had fallen several times. Avery had taken a flashlight, but he hadn't needed it, for the brightness of the snow was sufficient to illuminate the way downhill to the road through a thicket of pines, and to the van that was now looking like an igloo—there would be a lot of cleaning to do tomorrow, and he hoped his snow blower would fire up in the morning to clear the road. Paul had kept his head down all the way, and had never complained even when he fell down.

"Should be gone by tomorrow," Avery said, pointing at the sky. The snow was thinning and a patch of moon was appearing in the east.

"My iPad said so too. Before we lost the signal."

"Oh, yes—I forgot the iPad."

Avery sucked the icy air into his lungs and exhaled. "Do some deep breathing—it'll be good for you."

"My nostrils are frozen. Nothing's going in."

"Then breathe through your mouth."

"Only fish breathe through their mouths."

Avery put his arms around the boy and turned them back towards the house. He wasn't going to win any arguments tonight.

***

Now as he sipped a cup of cocoa in the warmth of the cottage, Avery thought back to happier times. The shape tucked inside the sleeping bag on the fringe of the glow from the fireplace could have been Damian as a boy, not Paul. And Pat would have been around then, putting the dinner things away, preparing the beds, getting the old cottage ready for the night and filling the place with her generosity and warmth. After she died, Avery had tried to get away from it all by selling the old cottage and building this new one, but remnants of the past were difficult to escape: the old couch, a recliner that knew every contour of his body, the books that had followed him throughout his life and shaped his character, the slumbering child in the sleeping bag one generation removed from the previous one. And the ghost of Pat who came back to him every night, fading increasingly with each visit and now locked into set images of times past. That was the problem: there were no new images; Pat was frozen in history. She could not grow old alongside him as he lurched into his uncertain future.

***

They dug out the next morning, or rather he dug out while Paul sat in the van after the snow had been brushed away from the sides and windscreen. The antifreeze he'd put in the snow blower's fuel tank had prevented blockage, the blower started after a couple of cranks, and Avery was able to clear the track around the van. Then he hitched his portable snowplough to the vehicle and cleared the track all the way to the main road two kilometres away. After Avery stored his survival implements back in the woodshed, they set out for the city.

"Can we stop at Tim Hortons?" Paul asked, typing away on his iPad as soon as they were out of the dead zone. Breakfast hadn't been that grand back at the cottage as Avery had forgotten to buy eggs. "There's a store five kilometres from here," Paul said, consulting his GPS. After a pit-stop for a couple of breakfast sandwiches and hot chocolate, Paul was busy again on his iPad. He spoke again only when they hit the outskirts of Toronto. "What do we tell Dad about last night?"

"There's nothing to tell. We were snowed in. We hunkered in and dug out this morning. A typical winter's sojourn in Canada. He's not used to this as we always took him to the family cottage in the summer."

When they pulled into the driveway, to Avery's surprise, it was Sylvana who opened the door. Avery had always admired his daughter-in-law's striking beauty, intelligence, and energy. Although she operated her business out of the home office most days, she wasn't dressed for work today; a one-piece track suit and running shoes were her only accoutrements. He remembered the indoor gym they had in the basement, but there wasn't the sweat of exercise on her, simply lines under her eyes. She focused her gaze on her son, eyes flashing. "You've missed school today."

Avery intervened while Paul visibly shrunk. "My fault, I took him away to the cottage to give you two some space. I forgot to check the weather report."

She looked at him for the first time and he saw guilt in her green eyes, not the flash of excitement or positivity, or anger that he was accustomed to seeing. She was the girl who liked to pose for family shots, link hands, and infuse smiles in everyone for the camera. Today she looked forlorn, like she was disappointing him. And yet, he was the guilty one for making her son lose a day of school. While they stared at each other, unable to form words to match this new situation, Paul brushed past both of them and ran indoors.

Avery remained on the porch steps; he hadn't been invited in, and now he felt he couldn't enter the house like before—relationships had changed.

"I hope you were able to work through things last evening with Damian."

"It's going to take a long time to reach a settlement. Your son is stubborn."

Your son? Not *my husband?*

"These are unusual circumstances. People behave differently. You can also write this divorce thing off as a bad project and go back to how it was before, for Paul's sake."

The green eyes flashed again, buried anger finally being released. "For Paul's sake? It's always for the children's sake. What about us? What about me?"

"It's *always* been about you. You and Damian. Now you can think of Paul for a change."

"You can tell that to *your* son. Except that he left this morning on a flight to Ottawa. Business, he said." The way she spat out the words made him wonder whether she doubted Damian's business dealings, whether he too was cheating on her on these "business" trips. No, he had to believe better of his son. He decided to push her.

"Well, at least he's not doing it on a laptop in full view of everyone in this house."

Sylvana looked like she had been slapped. But she held onto the door, regaining her composure quickly. "So, he's told you! And about five hundred other people. He'll be splashing it on Facebook next."

"Why did you allow yourself to get caught? Were you looking for help?"

Her shoulders drooped. "It was a moment of weakness. I wanted his attention."

"And you got his venom instead."

"There's too much bad blood between us now. We were ill-matched from the beginning. Going our separate ways is best."

"Are you sure?"

She did not reply but closed the door gently in his face.

***

When he returned home it was midday, and he made himself a sandwich and opened a can of beer. He switched on the radio, but the music did not dispel the silence that now enveloped this house, his home of the last twenty years. Pat's pictures still hung on the walls. They were together in some, at family barbecues with her large extended family in the Maritimes, at the church women's auxiliary to which she had been introduced by Lizzy and to which she had remained committed for many years, with Damian at his high school and university graduations. Everyone was smiling in these pictures, except in one, in which all those gathered were tense and formal: Sand Pharmaceuticals's twenty-fifth anniversary dinner party in 2001, featuring Pat and him in spiffy outfits, black tie for him and cocktail dress for her. Pat's normally radiant face was absent in that picture, replaced by a slight diffidence, even doubt. Perhaps she could sense the imminent danger to her husband in the man standing next to her in the photo: Martin Brock, recently promoted over Avery's head to COO after the introduction of Depo-Gen, the new generic version of the original Depo-Med, the generic that was supposed to keep Sand alive into the future. Avery had left that photograph on the wall for the perverse reason that it reminded him of his personal downhill spiral, which had kicked off

37

with Brock's arrival at Sand and went into accelerated mode after that twenty-fifth-anniversary event. He recalled the fateful executive committee meeting when the generic drug project had kicked off...

Norman Samuels had been in a particularly bad mood that day, poring over various documents as his executive team filed into the boardroom. It was a hot summer afternoon on a Friday in 1998, and everyone had been wondering why a meeting had been called at this time of the day when many preferred to be on the golf course, Samuels included. Brock, contrary to custom, made his appearance after everyone had taken their seats.

"Thanks for giving up your golf or cottage run, gentlemen," Samuels rasped as Brock began setting up a projector at the end of the room. "But this couldn't wait until next week. I want to head into the weekend with a resolution."

Everyone looked around. Mark Preston of HR had rings of sweat under his arms, and so did Sam Mukherjee, the controller. The others, the heads of R&D and Production, tried to look impassive yet engaged.

"Our quarterly numbers are not getting any better," Samuels said. "The question I want resolved today is generic drugs—do we get into them or not?" He nodded at Brock, who brought up a PowerPoint presentation on the screen opposite.

Mukherjee was the first speak, his Indian accent gaining prominence in his nervous haste. "With respect, Mr. Samuels...er...Norman, we have gone over the business case before. Generics will cut our margins by half."

Avery added, "Why are we revisiting old ground?" He was feeling irritated. It appeared that Brock, the sole proponent of pseudo-generic drugs from the time he had arrived at the firm two years ago, was doing an end run on the team.

"Look at the numbers Martin has come up with." Samuels nodded again to Brock.

Brock spoke for the first time, his greased hair gleaming in the closed room, its fragrance wafting towards his audience, a mixture of citrus and nervous sweat. "I've revised the strategy. We will not introduce the generic version when the original comes to the end of its shelf life, as originally planned. Instead, we will do it *earlier*, about three quarters of the way there. Thereby, we come to market with the generic version *ahead of* the generic drug manufacturers, and we get to dictate prices in that space. It will deter the generics from entering, because another generic, ours, already exists in that product category. Our costs of production are the same, as we use the same process that the brand-name version uses, and the same ingredients with a slight variation or two. Only the packaging is different—it's a terrific cost advantage over the generics who have to create a whole new production line."

"And how do you know this will work? Not financially, but ethically?" Avery asked. Avery's and Brock's head-banging was well known in the firm ever since Norman Samuels had introduced Brock to the executive team as "the up-and-comer from Alberta, brought in to shake up our complacency."

"I gave Martin the go-ahead a year ago with Miles and his R&D team to start working on a generic version of Demo-Med," Samuels said.

"You what—?" Avery's exploded and then quickly tried to recover. This was staggering news. And the rest of the team had been kept in the dark? Including Miles, who would occasionally join them for a drink down at Mick's, but had never mentioned this project?

Brock quickly launched into his PowerPoint, pulling up research papers, market statistics, and other data from around the world, from noted experts like Yi, Rockett, and Eswaran on how the licensing of pseudo-generic drugs had strengthened the dominant firm (the producer of the original) in the industry.

Avery countered, "And I can show you the work of other experts like Ferrándiz, Kamien, and Zang that will argue the opposite, that introducing a pseudo-generic drug is a subtle form of patent extension, and is anti-competitive."

The head of Production spoke up. "Martin's right about the production process. It's pretty much the same as we have today. It will be relatively easy to put in place."

"Then why the heck have we been dicking about with this for so long?" Now it was Samuels's turn to blow up, throwing his papers in the air. "Every time we've raised this subject over the last two years, it has been shut down by the purists in this group. Times are a-changing, gentlemen—drugs are being manufactured everywhere. Very soon the Chinese and the Indians will be the drug manufacturing centres of the world and we will be driven out of business. If we don't extend shelf life until our next discovery, we are done for. Miles—" Samuels turned upon the head of R&D— "when *will* we have our next Big One, the anti-inflammatory drug, ready to go?"

"Five years at best. We've been delayed on the second phase trials."

"Do you have any others in the pipeline?"

Miles was squirming in his chair. "The rest are in phase one trials." Then he quickly added, "We have three in phase one."

"So, we are potentially five years away from our next new product and possibly seven to eight years away from another, if any of those three in phase one get through. And who pays the bills if all our existing products are nearing the end of their shelf life?"

Avery bit his lip and looked at the head of R&D, who kept his eyes riveted to the table. Miles didn't look like he was going to get into the old debate again, which they had both lost when Brock had made his case, soon after his arrival, that R&D was killing them and that they should focus on quick-to-market products rather than on ground-breaker ones, like the aging Depo-Med that was heading into its fifteenth year. After all, best-sellers like Lipitor and Viagra came only once in a lifetime, and only to the big guys who had years of product life to play with and deep pockets to fund R&D.

Brock continued his presentation, wrapping up with a clear recommendation: if started now, the generic version of Depo-Med's trials could conclude as early as the year 2001, and they should launch that product soon afterwards. This would not only be the launch of a new product but the beginning of an innovative product extension business.

"I'm sold," Samuels said, and from his eagerness to bring the meeting to a close, Avery guessed there had been some prior "positioning" that had gone on between the president and Brock. The rest of the executive committee had been brought into this room only to be delivered the *fait accompli.*

Avery was determined to maintain his position, while the rest of his colleagues remained silent. "I think we need to give this a bit more consideration. There are not only pros in this venture, there are cons too. We have to consider our brand position, our supply chain, the cannibalization factor. This is not only about tossing a new product over the wall."

"I think there is no longer time for debate." Samuels rose, cutting off further discussion. "Martin, put the funding requirements together with Sam and have it in my office by mid next week. Have a good weekend, gentlemen."

After the launch of Depo-Gen was announced three years later, Martin Brock was appointed COO, a position Avery had been groomed for. When the towers fell in New York six months later, the stock market sank into gloom; only pharma and military stocks bucked the trend, buoying Samuels's decision that he had made the right choices for the future of Sand.

Chapter 5

The following morning, after his ritual of breakfast and the newspaper, Avery sat down to his email. There was one from John Dodds, inviting him to the next meeting of the local Sixty-Five Plus Club, so that he would get to meet the members and outline their "Be Driven to Your Vote" plan; attached to the email was a list of homes of people in the riding who were sixty-five or older, with phone numbers where available. Avery guessed he would be expected to call all of these people and arrange pick-ups for those who needed one on election day. Another email had arrived from Doug Sanders with the attached minutes of Stan's last campaign committee meeting.

Doug's email reminded Avery of Stan's comment about the campaign secretary's online dating activities. Avery's fingers automatically typed "Online Dating Sites." A flood of links came through, replete with pop-ups for Viagra sales and pornography. Scanning the free "samples" he felt his cock harden, and it pleased him. It had been a long time since he had indulged in sex, probably years, not since Pat's illness and subsequent death. He considered it a relief that he hadn't woken in the mornings with a hard-on for a very long time. The loss of his career and Pat's death had definitely moved him in another direction. And yet here were all these people having lots of sex and flaunting it online. And he was getting a rise from spying on them. He must have some dregs of passion left in him. He had let grieving take over too much of his life force and drain his libido.

He sifted through the sleazy hook-up sites to one that looked like it was serious: a subscription-based site called Golden, for "mature adults," where pairings were done based on "sophisticated computer algorithms." Taking the plunge, he registered. He had to provide his real name, upload a "recent" photo of himself, state his top three likes and dislikes, and answer a psychographic questionnaire. He was sweating by the time he completed the registration. Then he had to pay for a three-month subscription amounting to a hundred-and-fifty dollars. He hesitated, and thought about deleting the whole bloody thing. But some compulsion kept him going, and the next he knew, he was receiving a "thank you" for his payment and being invited through the portal to view potential "matches."

The women on display blew him away. Many were accomplished professionals in their forties, fifties, and sixties looking for that next adventure after the death or divorce of a life partner. Many were living alone with money in the bank, their own house, a comfortable job, and with children—if any— long having left the nest. Many were in his own riding! *Where have I been these last few years?*

Then panic gripped him. What if he corresponded with them online and later met one at the grocery store or at the Sixty-Five Plus Club? Women (and men) were reputed to never post a recent photo of themselves online. *I mean take this woman, for instance: who can say she's a grandmother when she doesn't look a day over forty!*

But he was too far invested in this venture by now to back out. He chose three women ages fifty-five, fifty-eight, and sixty respectively, all living outside the riding, but within the Greater Toronto Area. The fifty-five-year-old redhead was a recent divorcee with an adult son, the fifty-eight-year-old blonde was a retired teacher and childless, and the sixty-year-old brunette (*Brunette at sixty? Had to be dyed!*) said she had a large family and would like to retire but couldn't as yet. He had picked them in order of probability: the redhead looked the most promising as she was the youngest of his picks and had a son similar to his in age; the blonde looked like she would not have any family baggage and would come with a good pension; the sixty-year-old looked the least likely, given her age, the "large family," and the fact that her financial means must be strained if she couldn't contemplate retirement, but she had the prettiest face of all three and reminded him a bit of Pat. He wrote to their pseudo mailboxes provided by the dating site, carefully copying and pasting the same message to all three, so that he would not have to remember what he had said to each.

An ad popped up on the screen for a vegetable-based therapy that improved men's erections, a pill that had to be taken three times a day for a month to improve function. He thought he'd try that too; at least it wasn't Viagra. He had ideological issues with the pharmaceutical industry, no doubt, but that did not extend to the wholistic health industry. And if he was going to be committing to dating, he'd better be "dressed for the party." Delivery of the "supplies" was promised within twenty-four hours. He pulled out his credit card again,

All this had taken considerable time, and when he pushed his chair back and rose, it was lunch time. Well, it had been an interesting morning, one different from his usual mornings when the ghosts of the past had been his only companions.

The little parcel was delivered as promised the next day via courier, and Avery surveyed the beige capsules with some trepidation. Then he shook his head and took the recommended dosage. Nothing happened that evening and he spent his time puttering around the house going through the routine of cleaning, reading, doing laundry, and watching the political news on TV. He also decided to pack Pat's clothes that hung in her section of their closet and put them away in boxes down in the basement. After all, if he went ahead and invited a woman home, he wouldn't want her to think that he was living with a ghost. He caught himself in the mirror, and he looked agitated, guilty. *Are those damned pills working? Am I turning into a randy old man?*

The next morning, he woke with a giant erection that startled him. What was he to do with this? He had difficulty urinating as his erection held up right through the act. A side of him was secretly delighted that the pills were indeed working, and it hadn't taken a whole month! He made sure to take his next pill after breakfast.

And for breakfast, he decided to finish what was left of Lizzy's food parcel that was still in the fridge. He microwaved it and ate it with relish. Today was going to be a good day; he felt ebullient. He was scraping the dregs of dhal makhani into his mouth when the phone rang. Barbara Spencer's voice came through, but the phone didn't display the Sand address.

"Hi, Barbara. This is a pleasant surprise. Where are you calling from?" he blurted with satisfaction. Her tense voice soon brought him up straight.

"Avery, you asked me to call if I needed help. Is this a good time?"

"Sure. Glad you called. What can I do for you?"

"I started... I started letting go as you asked me to. And I'm a mess."

"Oh." He started groping for words of support. He wanted to explain the paralyzed mornings when he would wake up and stare at an empty wall. The sadness that had become a physical pain. But the words were stuck in his throat. He should have warned her about the after-effects of letting go when they had last talked.

"I couldn't go into work today and stayed home." Her voice had a quiver to it.

"Can I come over to chat? Or listen?"

"That would be... that would be lovely. You sure I'm not asking for too much?"

"No problem. I'll bring a bottle of wine and some tissues."

Her voice immediately brightened. "And I've got the chocolate. That's all I've been eating today."

***

She lived in an apartment in Don Mills now; gone was the three-storey estate bungalow in Vaughan that she and husband Bill had bought after their marriage twenty years ago. It must have fetched a good resale price. Avery shared the creaky elevator with an Indian couple and their baby in her stroller. A courier type tried to scurry in with his bicycle at the last minute, then decided to take the next elevator. The eighth-floor corridor smelled of stale spicy cooking, and the carpet needed an upgrade.

She glared at him through a crack in the door, as if checking for intruders, before slipping the chain clear and letting him in. There was a lot of stuff in the apartment, shrinking it in size: shoes, coats, ornaments, a grand piano, potted plants, wall shelves full of books; the contents of a larger house had been dumped into this holding space pending further orders for disposal, he guessed.

Barbara was not wearing the makeup he was accustomed to seeing her in at the office, and she looked older and lined without it, closer to his age; her eyes were puffy and red. She was dressed in a tee-shirt under an unbuttoned sweater, with baggy sweatpants, and when the sweater swung open Avery noticed that she wasn't wearing a bra.

He looked about for a seat. The couch was oversized for the living room, and it jostled against the piano.

"You'd better use the couch, it's the only decent seat in this place," she said, going into the kitchenette and returning with two wine glasses. He broke open the screw-top of the wine bottle and poured two glasses. She sat next to him on the couch. He could smell the shampoo in her hair; her body scent and proximity were unsettling, yet heady. Maybe those pills were working on him, for he suddenly had a strong desire to have sex. *Rip it off, spread it out, and go for it.* He shook his head and blinked his eyes, trying to focus on the present.

She downed half her glass in a single gulp and let out a suppressed sigh of relief, followed by a burp. "I could use more of that."

He topped her glass again. "Better go slow. Alcohol creeps up. Are your boys around?"

"No. They're both in residence—one at Waterloo and the other in Hamilton."

"Expensive years." He sipped his wine.

"Our home...the house...in Vaughan, sold last evening."

"That can be stressful. I haven't sold mine yet, and I'm dreading the day."

She downed her glass. "All our dreams...in that house. The boys each had their rooms in that place. Now they share the second bedroom in this place whenever they visit. And they come up with every excuse not to."

"You couldn't live a lie. I'm sure Bill couldn't either."

"The house sale going through did it for me. There is no going back."

"There usually isn't when you set these balls rolling." *That's why I've tried so bloody hard not to let Damian and Sylvana start any balls rolling. But they don't listen to an old man.*

"I can't even play the piano now. I can't get into the mood. I think I should get rid of it."

"Give it some time. They say music is good for the soul."

He spotted an audio remote control lying on the side table and switched it on. Light classical music, a song from *Phantom of the Opera*, began playing somewhere.

"'The Music of the Night' was our favourite piece," he said. "Pat and I saw that musical four times."

"Glad you like it. Bill and I saw the show in New York when we went there for our honeymoon." Her voice had lost its edge now, and she was sounding melancholy.

"Sorry, I didn't mean to stoke old memories." He made to switch the music off, but her hand on his restrained him. Her touch sent goose pimples up his arm. His groin stirred.

"Let it play. It allows us both to escape to a happier time." She drank more wine, and he did too. The song ended, and "All I Ask of You" began. The wine started to take hold.

She was looking into his eyes now, a hungry, lonely woman. And he, a lonely old man who had realized only in the last twenty-four hours that he too could still get hungry. "Lonely single people do stupid things when they're alone," she had said when they last met, but he was past caring now.

When their lips met, it came with no surprise or embarrassment. They were old colleagues crossing another line in their relationship with no corporate strictures to prevent them anymore.

Her emotional waves engulfed him, and he was the instrument stoking her fire. He lost himself in her kisses and caresses that verged on desperation, and they remained on the couch, clothing falling off bodies in stages, scared to rise and go into her bedroom lest that would break the spell. Ever the mentor to his protégée, he made sure that she achieved release before he gave into his needs. He was surprised at his self-control, conditioned from a lifetime of marital sex, despite that other, more recent urge pushing him to let fly like a stud bull in the afternoon. After the climax, they settled back on the couch, satiated, relieved that sex was not only enjoyable but achievable in a world where loneliness was the lot of the aging.

She rolled over on her side and drained the wine bottle into her glass. His first glass was still half-drunk. "That was the best goddamn fuck I've had in a long time!" she exclaimed, taking a swig and looking down at him with sultry eyes. "Pity you didn't teach me the ropes to lovemaking when I was working for you."

He liked the ego boost. He could actually *make* it with a much younger woman! "It wasn't in the job description." But now as the mojo drained out of him, he felt self-conscious and reached for his pants.

"Oh, oh, there you go. Wham, bang, thank you ma'am? What about the customary seconds?" She was giggling, but there was an ironic ring to her humour. *With a younger woman you've gotta go a second time!*

"I prefer the adage 'familiarity breeds contempt' or 'absence makes the heart grow fonder.'"

She rolled over to his side and began sucking on his ear, hot saliva spreading down the side of his face, her hand slipping between his legs, squeezing. He felt his cock stiffen again. *My God, this hasn't happened to me in a long time, a very long time. Those pills are bloody marvels!* Then he was mounting her again, determined to grab this erection that could vanish in an instant, penetrating, reaching deeper with each thrust as if it would be his last, while she parted her teeth in silent glee. He didn't come this time but she did, or appeared to, for she moaned louder than the first time, and when he rolled away from her, he was spent. He staggered to his feet and hobbled over to the washroom and closed the door, sinking on the toilet seat, exhausted but exhilarated, with a rapidly beating heart that felt like it might explode.

He showered, dried himself with her towel that smelled of that same shampoo, and returned to the living room. She lay sprawled on the couch, naked and snoring gently; she smelled of alcohol, sweat, and sex, and she looked attractive, a Botticelli nude, and he was embarrassed to find her enticing in that state of wanton abandon.

Today had indeed been an interesting day—a day of recaptured youth. He raised his half empty wine glass in a salute to himself and drained it.

He thought of quietly leaving the apartment while she slumbered. Perhaps they would be too self-conscious to resume a normal conversation after this impulsive outburst of passion. Perhaps it would be safer to continue the conversation by phone.

She awoke and her hands instinctively covered her breasts. Then she burst out laughing. "And you came over only to *talk?*"

He flushed deep, then chuckled. "There was some unfinished business to take care of first, it appears. From twenty years ago."

She pulled over a couple of cushions to cover her breasts and pubis and snuggled deeper into the couch, and when she spoke her voice was businesslike. "I actually wanted your advice on a matter. After I had gotten over my gloom, that is. . ."

He felt better now. This was the professional, unemotional area where he had spent most of his time with her in the past. "I'm all ears."

"Martin has asked me to head up the team that will be taking the company through its IPO."

So, you'll be working with our Damian. He kept his features impassive. "That's a high-profile assignment."

"What are the pitfalls?"

"The deal could fall through. And you'll be expected to fall on your sword."

"That's unlikely to happen, don't you think?"

"There's this rumour about the deaths linked to Depo-Med."

"Which is also my job to nullify."

"He's got a lot of trust in you. He promoted you to director soon after I left."

She twisted her mouth and for the first time he saw a trace of cruelty in her.

"He owes me a favour, or two."

"This job. . .it's important to you, isn't it? It defines you, doesn't it?"

"What else do I have when my children are ready to flee the nest, when I'm discarded by husbands and lovers—?"

"Lovers?"

She caught her blunder and her face blanched. And the picture became clearer to him. "You and Martin were an item?"

She pushed herself up from the couch. "I think I need a shower. I smell."

He followed her to the bathroom door. "When did that happen?"

As the jet of water hit her and she drew the shower curtain, her words slurred. "If you must know, soon after I found out about Bill, and at the time Martin was going through his second divorce. Three years ago. But it's over now. Office romances are high risk, we both were aware of it. The director job was his payoff to me." Her barely distinguishable words cut through him, making him want a refund of time, a refund of the last couple of hours at least.

She was obviously embarrassed to face him while making this admission, and the shower raised clouds of steam and increased in velocity. He was seething inside and didn't know how he would react when she emerged from behind the curtain. Of all people, Martin Brock! It indeed would be best that they carry on their conversation by phone.

He dressed quickly, and when the shower curtain did finally creak open, he was heading out the front door of the apartment.

***

She phoned him later that evening, and her voice was subdued. "I'm sorry, I didn't...I shouldn't have dragged my baggage onto the couch this afternoon."

"What's done cannot be undone. Thanks for being honest."

"Will I see you again? Things between us can't sit like this."

"I need some time to think. A lot has happened in the last three days since I visited Sand. I thought I was free of the place. I thought I was free of those people. I was wrong."

"I really am sorry. I don't need hurting you to be added to my baggage at this stage." Her voice sounded sufficiently penitent, so he decided to tell her what he had been mulling over.

"I think you should plan your exit strategy from Sand," he said.

"What? Now?"

"Yes. When companies privatize, shit happens, people lose jobs. You're going into a period of flux."

"Change can also provide opportunity, don't you think? You were a big opponent of change. That was your undoing at the firm."

"I'd been exposed to too much of it at the time, and I wanted the world to stand still, just for a little while."

"It doesn't."

"Anyway, you asked for my advice."

"Thank you. Can I keep in touch?"

"Yes."

"Thank you, again."

"You are welcome."

When he put down the receiver, he wondered whether he had been cruel. This was a woman adrift, grabbing at opportunities as they came her way. Was that wrong? Was he just one of those opportunities? An occasional fuck and a sounding board? If they had not been in today's pressure-cooker situation inside that apartment, would he and Barbara have been intimate? In future, would they go out to the theatre together, to dinner, take a walk, enjoy each other's company amidst the silences? Most importantly, would she come up and spend time with him at his cottage? He thought not. She was still embroiled in the corporate struggle, in the survival battle, in marital discord. He was beyond all this. He'd escaped from the human race. Or, had he?

He switched on his laptop and checked his email before retiring to bed. His eyes widened when he saw three email alerts to him from Golden. He logged into the site and went to his pseudo mailbox, and sure enough, his three ladies had all replied. *There is no escape from the human race.*

Pouring himself a mug of hot chocolate, he settled down to reply to each of them.

Chapter 6

Avery sat in the Starbucks cafe at the north end of the city, as he had been instructed to, reading the newspaper and awaiting his date: Sarah Brook, sixty, widowed, two adult children, Brian and Emily, four grandchildren between the ages of two and five, two apiece from each of her offspring. What was *not* right with this picture? A good story, a good Canadian middle-class story. Besides, all the children and their families lived within twenty kilometres of her home in North York. A happy family? He would see. . .

He was fifteen minutes early and had found a seat in the corner away from the busy counter, luckily, for the place was full of young people with laptops who never seemed interested in leaving, and whenever they did, they brandished Starbucks paper mugs like badges of courage, testaments to their employed-and-I-can-afford-to-drink-this-coffee status in life. The *Star* newspaper he was reading was uninteresting except for a paid column in the careers section announcing that Martin Brock had been appointed president and CEO of Sand Pharmaceuticals.

In a way, Avery was relieved that this would be the last of his "dates," and he was anxious for it to be over. Doug Sanders might be having his weekly romps via online dating, but Avery's own experiences so far had been fruitless. He had also discontinued taking his herbal erectile therapy. All he had achieved, other than for the Barbara episode, was a cramping urination problem with each morning's huge erection, an erection he'd stare at and mourn, "We're going nowhere, buddy. There are no ports left in this storm." He threw the packet of pills in the garbage. *Let me age gracefully, and let my erection fall where it may on that continuum.*

The fifty-five-year-old divorcee, whom he had met last week, had been vivacious and friendly until he had asked her about her previous marriage. The woman had then flown into a rage, beginning with "I'm suing the bastard for all he's got..." It was downhill after that, a bitter outpouring from a soul not yet ready to put the past behind. The fifty-eight-year-old retired teacher had been no better: she lived *only* in the past; she rhapsodized throughout their meeting over a trip to Italy she had taken with the only love of her life, twenty years ago (the man had never married her and had subsequently passed away), and she was determined that her new man, whoever that was to be, should spend a few weeks in Tuscany with her every year. Avery had not called either of the women back.

He spotted her entering and looking carefully around the cafe. He recognized her immediately from her online photo; at least she had been honest in this regard. He stood and waved. She recognized him too—he had also been honest—and came over.

"Avery?" There was laughter and openness in her eyes. "So nice to finally meet you, after all those emails."

"Likewise, Sarah." As she sat and placed her handbag at her side, he appraised her: brunette hair with a few grey wisps, chiselled features going soft, an upright bearing. She was dressed in a navy pantsuit, well cut, with no sign of the dreaded middle-age spread trying to disfigure it. Then he began to sweat; at these close quarters, she looked even more like Pat— Pat before the cancer ate her away. *My God, are we given a second chance?*

"Can I get you something? A coffee?" he offered before sitting down.

"Oh yes, I forgot, one is supposed to drink something, isn't one? A chai latte, then. But please ask them not to shout my name aloud."

They both laughed. "Maybe I'll give our names as Anthony and Cleopatra."

When he returned with the refreshments, she was writing in a greeting card. "Thank you. I thought I would fill the unforgiving minute by writing a card to my son, Brian. It's his birthday next week."

"I have to tell you that I'm quite inexperienced at this online dating thing," he said, as she put away the card.

"So am I. But my daughter, Emily, insisted. She met her husband that way. Emily set it all up for me. She filtered out the undesirable emails and sent me only the worthy prospects."

"You mean, Emily read my emails?" He started to blush.

She smiled. "I hope that doesn't embarrass you. She highly recommended you, though."

He couldn't erase the blush easily. "Warn me the next time I meet Emily. I'll run and hide." Why was he talking about a "next time" already? But this woman was making him relax, and he was beginning to enjoy her company.

After that, the conversation flowed freely between them and the hours slipped by without either of them noticing. The coffee shop emptied of lunch-goers and filled again with afternoon-break customers. Their drinks gave way to sandwiches, which they munched on as they recounted their life stories.

He was able to piece together her story from the various subjects they jumped to at random. She had studied law but never practised it. Her husband, Barry, had been a criminal lawyer turned provincial court judge, they had relocated often whenever he was appointed to different circuits, and she had supported his career. That, and raising two small children, had kept her rooted to the home. Afterwards, in her mid forties, with the kids boarded in Toronto, and while living in North Bay, she had obtained her teaching certificate and taught English in a rural school. Brian was now a lawyer and Emily was an assistant professor of English literature. Sarah's teaching career had been short-lived, for Barry developed pancreatic cancer ten years earlier. Sarah moved back to Toronto with him, but he passed away three years later. When she mentioned Barry, a tenderness arose in her face, and he understood that. It made it easy for him to talk to her about Pat.

They ordered another round of coffee and chai to wash down the food.

Avery decided to be bold and ask the question that had been bothering him. "You know, I was intrigued by your statement 'I would like to retire but cannot'—yet it sounded like you were having a lot of fun at whatever you were doing."

She smiled. "About five years ago, with Barry's death behind me, I did something adventurous. Something I'd always wanted to do. I opened a bookstore. 'Brook's Books' sounded like a wonderful idea."

"A bookstore? With everything going online?"

"I wanted it to be more than a Starbucks, where you had to bring your own stories in order to enjoy coffee and tea. I wanted a place surrounded by stories where people could enjoy their brew."

"And have you had fun?"

She looked pensive. "Yes and no. I achieved the dream, no doubt, but it's tough to make a go of the place financially. I introduced gifts and greetings cards. Now I have excess inventory to get rid of before I can transition ownership or shut the place down. You should come and visit sometime. We serve better coffee."

"I certainly will. Do you have a website?"

"No. I wish I could do some online marketing, but I have enough on my hands simply managing the place." She wrote down the address for him. "Well, I must be going. Gosh, it's got dark outside."

"I didn't notice the hours go by."

"Me, neither. You will come, won't you." The look in her eyes told him that she did like him, and that she may have been let down in the past by other men on Emily's prospect list.

"I will, for sure. How about Friday afternoon?"

"Great. And I'll make sure to have the latte available with one sugar and some cinnamon on the top."

"Thanks for observing."

***

When he got home, there was a message waiting for him. Barbara had called. He hadn't been in touch since the day of their sexual encounter three weeks prior, and he was feeling guilty about not phoning her. But there had been other women, closer to his age, who had been popping up on the scene, thanks to Golden.

She sounded relieved to hear from him. "I thought you had dumped me."

"I was busy with the election and all," he lied.

"I didn't call to make a date," she hurriedly said, putting him at ease. "I wanted to run something by you."

"Shoot."

"Remember Abbottan Labs?"

"How can I forget?" Abbottan had been Sand's closest competitor in the anti-allergenic space.

"Their HR department called me about a job. Head of Marketing. They'd been keeping tabs, especially after our most recent bloodletting."

"Bloodletting?"

"Martin wasted no time in cleaning house the minute he was in the president's office."

"Oh no."

"Yes. The cuts were deep this time. Old Olga got the chop too."

"She mentioned that she was going to be part of the next round."

"Martin had our outsourced HR company do it, and they were not compassionate in the least. Some employees who were travelling or on vacation got fired by email. The place is like a morgue."

"These things are not easy. Tell me about Abbottan."

"Can we discuss it over a glass of wine?"

When he hesitated, she quickly stepped in and her voice sounded disappointed. "Sorry, that was a trick question."

"I know where wine leads us."

"Is that wrong? We aren't cheating on anyone, are we?"

"No, I guess not. Let's do this. I've always wanted to drive you out to my cottage sometime. We'll have plenty of time to discuss things in private there."

They agreed on the coming Saturday.

***

On Friday, he visited Brook's Books.

The shop was located in a side street off Yonge, but within the busy North York shopping area. The first thing that hit him was the lighting and decor. The place resembled a magic cave with glittery stars, quarter moons, goblins and witches on broomsticks painted on indigo walls. The lighting was recessed, soft, and projected onto the walls. Bookshelves were embedded inside papier-mâché caves that reached out into the room, and there were plenty of chairs around an elevated centre, where it looked like readings and other literary happenings were staged on a regular basis, for a sign announced four reading events over the next two weeks. Two assistants, wearing purple Brook's Books tee-shirts, were helping young readers find their choices. Children's and YA books dominated the ground floor, and a staircase at the back had a sign that said "Adult Literature Upstairs." Traversing the darkened Disneyesque ground floor, he found the coffee shop in the adjoining room around the corner, a brighter area where most of the human activity seemed to be concentrated. Sarah was behind the coffee counter serving customers.

She saw him, waved, and shifted a stray curl of hair from her face. He walked up to the counter and sat on a bar stool. Cookies, cakes, and candy of all kinds, some looking home-made, jostled for space with coffee mugs and trinket displays along the counter.

"Thanks for coming. Your latte is brewing." Her face had lit up on seeing him, and he was starting to feel at home already, despite the other patrons who were either massed at the counter or occupying the four small tables in the room.

"Mmm! This is delicious," he admitted, sampling from the steaming and frothy mug she placed in front of him. "Beats the last place we were at."

"Goes well with a piece of apple strudel that I made yesterday," she said, placing a generous helping of the dessert on a plate beside his coffee.

He ate the strudel and drank his coffee, not in a hurry to finish either, content to watch life go on around him. *And I wanted to escape?*

"I might be a while," she said apologetically, tightening her apron. "We've had a rush today."

"I must have brought you good fortune. Take your time. I'm in no hurry." But she was already at the other end serving customers.

He studied her as she went about her business. She was handling many transactions at the same time: taking cash from a departing customer; removing used plates from the counter; putting fresh packs of coffee in the large, stainless-steel coffeemaker, which spewed heady aromas; serving cake, strudel, muffins, cookies; all with a smile that rarely left her face.

He recalled Pat at the bake sales when she would be serving hordes of churchgoers and seniors—crabby customers most of them, who loved to complain instead of accepting what was on offer—and she too had been always accommodating with a smile, letting complaints bounce off her broad shoulders. These women, Pat and Sarah, they only wished to see the good in life. Their lives, buttressed by caring husbands, had been shielded from the intrigues of broader human society, from the criminals that Barry must have faced in court, or the Martin Brocks and Norman Samuelses of the world that had been Avery's lot.

The thought of Brock and Samuels brought back a memory. He tried to stifle it and focus instead on the bustle of his surroundings. The smell of coffee usually reminded him of employees sitting around and drinking copious amounts of java when a layoff was imminent. During those times, computer hard drives were wiped clean of personal stuff and email, bookmarks were deleted, CMY (cover-my-ass) papers were ferreted away, and incriminating documents were shredded. Mindless chatting was accompanied by frenetic laughter during the waiting, and bad jokes—even rude ones—were de-rigueur, fuelled by the excess of caffeine. The aroma of coffee always brought out these thoughts of impending doom in Avery. But today, the composite smell of coffee, cake, and comfort food inside Brook's Books was not threatening. Instead, he was being lulled into a sense of placidness which allowed that other memory to surface...

Samuels had summoned him into his office, mid-morning, during the fall of 1996. The leaves had been falling in the backyard when he left for work that day; Avery had often wondered why falling leaves remained connected to that meeting in the president's office.

"Avery, come in." Samuels had been particularly ebullient, the mauve striped tie sitting solidly on his neck as if he'd just put it on, when usually, by this time of day, his top button would be undone, his tie pulled down, and his sleeves rolled up. "I wanted to introduce you to our latest addition to the...ah... family."

The man who had been sitting opposite Samuel's voluminous desk stood up and turned towards him. Sleek black hair, black shirt open at the neck, no tie, a blue blazer, tan slacks, and brown brogues setting off an athletic figure. It was the eyes that disturbed Avery: dark pools of luminosity that were unsmiling, and thin lips parted to reveal pearly teeth in what was to be interpreted as a smile.

"Martin Brock. Please to meet you." The voice was nasal, affected.

"Our new VP of Product Development, Boyd's successor." Samuels said triumphantly. "I thought you two should meet before I introduced Martin to the rest of the executive team."

"Welcome," Avery said, shaking Brock's hand, which was dry and strong.

"Sit down, gentlemen," Samuels said, going back to his plush armchair. "I'll make this brief before I take Martin around to meet the others, and for a tour of the facilities."

Avery sat in the second visitor chair across from Brock, facing the president.

"As you know, Avery, we have been too focused on R&D and in bringing our own products to market. With Boyd's retirement, and the entry of the generics into Canada, we need to rethink that strategy."

"We've discussed this before," Avery gently reminded his boss.

"Yes, and that's why in my search for a new head of Product Development, I have been looking for someone with a fresher vision. We are all too entrenched in this company to have that vision. We like the tried and true. And yes, I know what you're about to say to me—it has worked for us in the past."

Avery sat back. Trying to interrupt Samuels when he was getting warmed up was counter-productive.

"Martin comes from the generics sector and I was intrigued by his thoughts on short cycle, multi-replicable drugs. That is: how to beat the generics at their own game."

"But we've always kept ourselves above that horde."

"There's money to be made in that 'horde's' playing field." Brock spoke up for the first time.

"Yes," Samuels said. "And that's why I want Martin to come up with a plan to take on the generics who are eating our lunch. I don't mean to abandon brand-name and leap into generics wholeheartedly. I want to have them both in our stable and synergize off each other. I trust that the two of you, Marketing and Product Development, will work cooperatively to see us realize that strategy."

The pointed look Samuels aimed at Avery gave him no option but to stand up and extend his hand to Brock. "You have my support. Welcome aboard."

"I'm looking forward to it." Again, those unflinching eyes, surveying, categorizing, sensing whether this was an ally or an obstacle to be ground out of the way.

Avery had left the meeting feeling trapped.

"You seem lost." Sarah had arrived in his corner once again and was removing her apron. "We'll be closing shortly, so we could go for a walk, or a drink, if you like."

"Uh. . .I was so comfortable, old memories came rushing back."

"Pleasant ones, I hope."

"Ones I can't shake. Not all of them are pleasant. Yes, I'd like that drink."

She gave him a tour of the bookshop before they left. The adult section upstairs was a mess, with many old titles and books in disarray. "This is the area I need the most help with. I don't make enough to hire help for upstairs *and* downstairs, and customers litter things."

"Why not shut the adult section down, sublet the space upstairs, and focus on kids' books and the coffee shop?"

She looked at him askance. "Hmm, I never viewed it that way."

"I learned about focus and specialization in business school."

They returned downstairs, where she replaced a few books that had been left lying around and then closed up for the night.

They found an Italian restaurant a short walk away and settled down to a carafe of wine.

The alcohol helped him talk. "I didn't recognize that the corporation was a second wife to me. I've been grieving two deaths over these last five years."

"Barry took his job seriously too. He would be a torn man during trials, especially the ones that involved rape or domestic violence."

"There was a recent downsizing at my old firm, and it triggered memories of my own exit. I wasn't ready to leave, I guess, and now I'm too old to get back and finish what I started."

"You need a clean break, a change of scene."

That's when he told her about his cottage.

"That's sounds wonderful! I loved our life when Barry was on circuit. Country life was the best. The solitude, the fresh air, the time to think, to create. I'd like to visit sometime."

"You will." He suddenly remembered that he had made an appointment to go there tomorrow with Barbara. He averted his eyes and concentrated on his wine, hoping she would not push any further in that direction for now.

Instead, she surprised him by saying, "I'd like to invite you to the party I'm organizing for Brian, next week. You'll get a chance to meet my family, and the grandchildren."

"Isn't that a bit sudden? We've just met."

Her eyes were open, trusting. "At our age, we don't have all the time in the world, do we? And we've faced many embarrassments too. It doesn't bother me. That is, if you're comfortable with it."

"I'd love to come." he reached out and took her hand. It was warm and comforting and she let it lie in his, smiling, kind. "Thanks."

When they left the restaurant and he had accompanied her to her white Honda Civic, he opened his arms to say goodbye and she returned the intimacy by giving him a warm hug and a peck on the cheek. "I'll email you directions to the party," she called out as she pulled her car away. This time the peck didn't come with an accompanying dose of lust, as it had done with Barbara on the day he had visited Sand; this time he recognized the touch of an old friend, someone he had probably known in another life.

Chapter 7

They left early the following morning and made it to Peterborough for a late breakfast. He had asked Barbara to come prepared for bad weather, although the forecast was calling for clear skies but colder than usual temperatures. Avery had stocked up on groceries before leaving Toronto.

Barbara was in a cheerful mood and had been dressed and waiting for him when he arrived at her apartment. She had surprised him by bringing more than what he thought was needed for a brief visit like this: she piled a suitcase of clothes and two heavy sweaters in the back seat. She was dressed in a body-hugging ski suit with a parka and a black headband around her golden hair. No wonder she excelled in her job—always anticipating the unexpected!

He tried to keep the conversation general during the drive, but they invariably drifted back to Sand. Their shared experiences at the firm were easy connections to draw on when conversation slumped.

"Do you ever think of coming back into pharmaceuticals? Even as a consultant?" she asked him.

"It's too late now. My sharpness has deteriorated. Besides I've lost all my contacts in the marketing world. If I can believe their Linked In profiles, most of them have moved on."

"But you miss the challenge, no?"

"Yes. I do. Only yesterday, I was recalling how I met Brock for the first time."

Her voice dropped a tone. "And you still harbour hurt feelings about him?"

"Well, I suppose I should move on. But I find it objectionable how he and Norman secretively set up a subsidiary company to trial the generic drugs that Sand came out with subsequently. It was all hush-hush, while the rest of us on the executive team were opposed to jumping on the generics bandwagon. There were other things too…"

"Like?"

"He cast a spell on Norman that made him the chosen one."

She laughed. "You're jealous."

"I learned, only later, what quicksand we had built our corporate lives on."

"And you're pissed off that I was more than an employee to him once."

"To be honest—yes."

"But it's over now, Avery. You've got to put that one behind you too. Practise letting go yourself."

They drove the rest of the way in silence. Midway, she slipped a CD into the van's player and "The Music of the Night" played quietly, but it did not have the same magic as the last time he had heard it.

At the cottage, the lake was frozen under a cloudless sky. A thin layer of snow had fallen overnight, creating perfect cross-country skiing conditions, and a few skiers were already out following the ribbon of white that was a tributary of Elk Lake winding its way through the woods. He sensed that they would be uncomfortable in their forced isolation and would need a distraction. After depositing their bags inside the cottage, he decided to show her around the property.

"This is my self-contained, off-grid refuge," he said, spreading his hands out in the front yard. "Over here is my well that pumps drinking water." They skirted the well and walked to the other end of the property where the septic tank was located. "I dug the septic myself. I wanted to be responsible for burying my own shit, you might say."

She laughed and seemed amused by his enterprise around the place. "You think you could live here year-round without going insane?"

"I'm certainly going to give it a try."

He took her around the cottage to the eastern end of the property and to a clearing where four solar panels provided electricity. "And if all breaks down on me, there's a plentiful supply of wood to keep me warm throughout the winter," he said, gesturing to the trees that hemmed them in on three sides, the fourth side dropping down to the lake.

He noticed that she was showing signs of boredom by the time they had rounded the shed, the gazebo, and the herb garden, which lay forlorn in the winter freeze. He suggested a cross-country ski if she was up to it. She nodded tentatively, and he took that for agreement, and immediately went back to the shed to fish out skis. "I've got many pairs stored here— from Damian's as a kid, to Pat's, to mine, and to some I picked up at a garage sale. You never know when they will come in handy." They found a pair that fitted her, Pat's, and they skied around the icy lake, waving to the occasional skier coming along in the opposite direction. She was not a good skier and fell a couple of times on the turns. The weather was bracing in the extreme, chafing lips and cheeks, and threatening to break through any crack in their parkas. Avery found it invigorating, the icy air penetrating lungs, gripping muscles in its vise, taxing endurance, forcing a survival response. They exited the lake onto the frozen river, and a kilometre out Barbara started developing cramps, signalling for him to turn back. Disappointed, he complied. He helped her half-ski, half-walk back to the cottage.

"Brr!" she rubbed her hands vigorously as he stoked the fire to life back inside the living room. They had shed their parkas by the door and thrown blankets around themselves to warm up. When the fire got to a steady roar, he uncorked a bottle of Merlot and opened a tin of crackers. He had bought selections of cheeses and cold meats for accompaniment. They curled up on the couch.

"How's the cramping?"

"It's easing. I could do with a good massage." She had a "I feel neglected" look.

He couldn't be aloof anymore. "I'm at your service."

First, he applied an ice pack, then he massaged her calves with a liniment lotion. She responded easily to his touch and eased back on the couch, sighing. "Oh, I could submit to this forever. Don't stop."

His libido started rising (*who needed those damned pills?*), and he broke away this time before matters got out of hand again. He wrapped her calves in another blanket and resumed his seat next to her.

"You do know how to take care of a woman, Avery."

He smiled and sipped his drink. "I've had lots of practice. With one woman."

After the second glass of wine, and sufficiently warmed up, she said, "You know, for all the winters I spent with my family up in Ottawa, I must admit I'm a city girl."

"Didn't you enjoy our recent exercise in the great outdoors?"

"Sure—but only with you being there to keep me going. I wouldn't have done it on my own. I would have preferred to hole up in my apartment playing piano—or trying to play it, I should say—on a cold day like this."

She had answered his question: if he was planning to live here on a permanent basis, she wouldn't fit into that picture. Perhaps it was best. It made the previous day's visit to Sarah more real, less duplicitous. He decided to get to her unasked question.

"You wanted to talk to me about Abbottan Labs?"

"Should I take the job? It's come at a most inconvenient time."

"The IPO?"

"Yes. I can't let Martin and the firm down."

"He will have no hesitation in letting you down when it suits him."

"It hasn't happened yet."

"I say, take the new job. Although you'll miss the chance of working opposite my son, Damian Morgan."

She gulped. "Damian?....Morgan?... but of course—"

"Do you remember the gangly kid who came to the firm for Kids to Work day those many years ago?"

"He had your last name then."

"He changed it to his mother's on social media to remain anonymous and then found out that it had become his identity, especially when he started networking with the Bay St. types while he was articling, so he legally changed his surname to Morgan."

"I'll keep it our secret from Martin."

"I was going to ask that of you next. But you won't have to, if you take the Abbottan job."

"You really want me to leave the old firm, don't you?"

"It's no longer the *old firm*. Don't you see that? Or are you the proverbial frog in the cauldron?"

They drank more wine and she snuggled up beside him, but the spark that had ignited them the last time was gone. They were more like old friends sharing a reminiscence. A heavy sadness hung between them, a promise of something deeper that was now stillborn. Eventually, the recent exercise, the wine, and the sense of impending separation made them doze as the fire simmered lower.

Her cell phone rang, jolting them both from their slumber. She immediately grabbed it and, recognizing who it was, slipped into the bedroom and shut the door. He heard her agitated voice and the wooden floor creaking with her pacing.

She emerged ten minutes later. "Could we drive back tonight?" she asked. "The weather is clear."

"I can take you back." He was grateful to whoever had called. The prospect of a night with Barbara would have been going in the wrong direction, much as the sex would have been interesting, if there was indeed going to be sex; but after this morning, he wasn't sure, and he didn't want to find out. "Any problem back at home?"

"Martin wants to meet me. It's over the due diligence we've been doing to get the IPO underway. Your Damian and his team have been raising all sorts of questions."

Avery sighed. "Trust our Martin to spoil things, especially on an employee's day off. And you'd better not call him 'Avery's Damian' in front of Brock."

She smiled. "Well, you revealed the shocking truth!"

He lifted her suitcase, which still lay unopened, and placed it on the landing outside the front door. Then he grabbed his key and threw on his parka. "I'm ready when you are."

***

"I'm sorry this visit didn't work out, Avery," she said as he steered the car down the narrow trail to the main road.

"It was meant to reveal some truths. And it did. I'm too old for you. I'm too full of old garbage while you still have optimism in you, and you need to preserve that."

"I can't take the Abbottan offer. That much became clear to me while we were talking, but thanks for the advice. Taking Sand public and being part of that venture is too much for me to pass up on. Like you, I've invested too much in this company. We have both been marked 'Made in Sand.'"

"All the best, then! You can call on me if you need to pick my brains from time to time."

Then she surprised him with a question that came out of the blue. "So let me pick it now: do you remember Hank Smith?"

"Sure. There would be no Depo-Med without old Hank."

"Whatever happened to him?"

"Hank was credited with the invention of Depo-Med, although Sand held the patent as his employer. He kind of vanished from the scene one day. We were told that he had taken early retirement and headed out west. We found out later that Hank was moved over to the generics subsidiary that Norman set up, the secret operation that we were not privy to. I believe he ran the clinical trials for the generic version of the drug. And after the generic drug came out on the market, he departed for parts unknown—he wasn't even present at the launch press conference. I guess

69

he was fed up with the game too. I was kind of disappointed that he never kept in touch with any of us afterwards. I would have loved to have picked his brains over a pint at Mick's. Why do you ask?"

"Premier Investments is asking for a statement from Hank on his tenure as chief scientist for the firm as part of their due diligence process. Martin has a brief on Hank that he wants to go over with me before releasing it to Premier. I thought I'd get your version of the facts first before I met with Martin."

"You shouldn't be telling me this."

"I know. It's a muddle, isn't it? Sometimes I'm so in over my head with these things. Let's talk about something else. Tell me about the latest movie you watched. . ."

They got off onto safer subjects until they were back in Toronto. It was past 10 p.m. when he pulled up opposite her apartment building. The street was deserted except for a black SUV parked with its engine running on the opposite side of the street.

Barbara drew in her breath as soon as she caught sight of the vehicle. "Don't stop here!" she hissed. "Pull around the corner to the parking garage."

Too late, he had already braked in front of the entrance to her building.

"Go!" she nearly yelled at him, and he pulled away again, going around the driveway to the entrance of the underground parking garage. She rifled in her handbag and pulled out a bunch of keys. In the rear-view mirror, he saw the SUV pull away from the curb.

He paused in front of the metal doors while she clicked on her key fob. The garage doors creaked opened slowly. "These blasted doors— what fucking security!" she said. "Go, go, go!"

Too late, the SUV had pulled up on their tail and slid in easily behind them before the garage doors began their reverse trajectory.

"Who the fuck is that?" Avery was slowly getting the picture.

"Drive around." She had ducked her head so as not to be visible to the driver behind. "When you get around the next corner and out of sight of the SUV, I'm going to jump out of the van and scoot away between some vehicles. You keep driving and leave by the same entrance. The garage doors will open automatically to let you out. You can bring my bags to me tomorrow."

"Hang on!" Avery accelerated with a squeal of rubber and took the bend quickly, then he raced down two more floors and braked. Barbara wrenched the passenger door open, jumped out, and crouched between two parked cars. He reached across, pulled the passenger door shut, and accelerated down to the third and final floor of the garage before commencing his ascent towards the exit ramp, hoping he had bought some time for Barbara to make it back into her apartment safely. During this burst of activity, he had lost sight of the SUV. Should he call the police? Don Mills wasn't the safest of neighbourhoods and this seedy building must teem with all sorts of hoodlums.

When he made it back up to the exit doors there was only one obstacle before him: the SUV stood blocking his exit. So, it hadn't followed him at all! Its lights dipped and flashed in his face. He pulled the van to a halt, nose to nose with the obstructing vehicle, and flashed and dipped his own headlights in response while wondering who would tire of this stand-off first. He reached for his cell phone and was about to dial 911, when the lights in the SUV went out and its driver-side door opened.

The figure caught in the van's headlights had thickened since Avery had last seen him. But Martin Brock looked sharp in his black overcoat and polished brogues, hair slicked back, not a strand out of place. He walked over to Avery's side window and tapped with a black leather-gloved hand. Avery rolled down his window.

"Hello, Avery—fancy meeting here!" The moustache had some grey flecks now and the jowls were heavy and lined. "Dropping off someone?" Brock was peering into the vehicle, eyes straying briefly over the two women's sweaters tossed over the rear seat. "Funny, I was picking someone up myself."

"None of your damned business, Martin." Avery's breath clouded the air between him and Brock.

"Still sore over the past?" The tone was nasal to the point of hilarity.

"You're blocking my exit and its freezing in here."

"Thought I saw you with someone we both knew."

"You must be mistaken. When I'm ready to talk, I'll call and set up a better time and location. Now, can you please back your vehicle out and let me leave?"

"You do that, Avery. I'd love to shoot the shit sometime. Under better circumstances. Perhaps at Mick's."

With a leering grin, Brock headed back to his vehicle and moved it out of the way.

As soon as the garage doors swung open again, Avery shot out and up the ramp, feeling thwarted, angry, and beaten, like he had felt the last time he had seen Brock, on the day the COO and the president had had their little "severance talk" with him, with Olga Beckmeyer waiting in the anteroom ready to escort him out of the building. And there hadn't been the heightened smell of coffee to alert him on that occasion either.

***

"Shoot the shit"—Brock had actually invited him to do that? Avery gripped the steering wheel tightly as memories of the last time they had "shot the shit" came back to him. It had been at Mick's bar, during Brock's early days in the company, in the spring of 1997, when the two heads of Marketing and Product Development were sizing each other up and trying to form the harmonious working relationship the CEO had ordered them to develop. Avery had been trying to acculturate Brock to Sand's habits, and drinking at Mick's after a gruelling day was one of them. After many excuses, Brock had finally relented and joined him for a drink after work.

As soon as they sat down, Brock had drunk at a fast clip, out-drinking Avery two to one. Right through the rapid guzzling of beer, Brock stared at the hockey game on the TV where the Leafs were losing again.

"Are you happy working here?" Avery finally prompted, after he had finished his second and final beer for the evening.

Brock stared down at his stein, his lower lip sagging, as if it would dribble shortly. "This is an incremental company. It will never be great. I think I made a mistake."

"Incremental is good, as long as the trajectory is upward."

"I came from an incremental family, I would've been stuck in redneck, small town Alberta if I hadn't broken away and made it on my own terms."

"I stayed in my family for as long as I could. I had a happier upbringing than my parents ever did."

"Ever heard of S curves and disruptive technologies?"

"Sure, B-school stuff. Depo-Med was one of *my* S curves."

"But it's coming to the top end of its S. We need another S. Many more S's."

"Usually, one S is all you need to build your career."

"And you guys are hanging on to your Depo-Med—your solitary S—for dear life, and suppressing everything—and everyone—else."

"There are other products in Sand's pipeline, but they need to go through their due process in the testing phases."

"I have no time to wait."

"Then you are in the wrong industry. The software industry might suit you better. This internet buzz is cannibalizing business models by the hour."

"Watch me! There will be more S curves. In pharma."

"There will be, no doubt. But we can't circumvent regulations in order to get there."

"What you *show* the bureaucrats and what you *do* to make a buck don't have to be the same. Why don't you use those positioning skills that you guys are so good at in Marketing to get us to market faster?"

"Unfortunately, there is no place in drug testing for positioning."

"Agh, this is a futile argument. I hate those guys in Ottawa. Piss on them." He downed his drink, belched, and staggered towards the toilet. By the way Brock lurched forward forcefully, like a punch-drunk boxer, Avery was convinced that had a Health Canada inspector strayed across his colleague's path at that moment, the poor official would have been run over and ended up in a stream of urine.

A week later, Norman Samuels convened the initial management team discussion on generic drugs, and Martin Brock presented his first PowerPoint business case to support the discussion.

Chapter 8

Avery was impatient to get to Sarah's house for the party the following Saturday. The week in between had been one of ups and downs.

He had visited the Sixty-Five Plus Club, as promised, and met with John Dodds. The gathering had been a large one of over eighty people. What had drawn them was the subsidized five-dollar lunch, sponsored by a generous, unnamed Centrist Party donor. John had outlined the service being provided in the way of transportation to the polling booths. There was a sign-up sheet for those needing a ride.

A senior in the front row, leaning heavily on his walker and who seemed a bit hard of hearing, rose and tottered on his feet. "Where are you going to pick us up from?"

John went to the microphone. "As mentioned, if you live in an apartment building, we will pick you up in the lobby at the appointed time. If you live in a private dwelling, we will come to your front door."

After the sign-ups were completed, lunch was served, followed by bingo. Avery excused himself at this point. John stopped him on the way out and said, "We've got over forty people needing rides. Looks like we'll be busy. I'll print out a route map and a pick-up schedule, and parcel out the rides between our volunteers. I hope you're able to make two or three runs on election day."

"Sure. I'm happy to do that."

***

The following evening, Barbara called. "Avery, did you get off okay that evening? Sorry for the cloak and dagger. But it would have been awkward if Martin had seen us together."

"He said hello at the exit doors."

"Omigod! You ran into him?"

"He was blocking my way. He stepped over to talk."

"Did he mention me?"

"No. But I'm not sure what he picked up. Your sweaters were in the back seat."

"Oh, shit! Well, I won't be wearing them to the office for a while. Better yet, keep them with you. But can you drop off my suitcase tonight?"

"You're sure he wouldn't be outside your building again? Guarding his property? I didn't call you because I thought your phone would be tapped."

"Oh, don't be over-dramatic. Saturday night was a fluke. When he said he wanted to discuss the brief, I didn't think he would be actually coming over. He later said he didn't trust email with such confidential papers."

"Did he ask you about me?"

"Never said a word. But you know Martin. He keeps his cards close."

"And how was the brief?"

"Pretty innocuous stuff. Years of employment, credentials, papers written, significant discoveries, research methodology. I don't think anything was written by Hank himself. Martin must have copied and pasted the information from our archives."

"I'll drop off your suitcase this evening. But I won't stay."

***

Two days later he called Damian to check on his son's evolving domestic situation. Avery was feeling guilty for brushing him off that evening in the van while driving up to the cottage with Paul.

He called the number at Premier Investments during business hours. His son was his usual official self, detached, dry. No trace of resentment from their last encounter surfaced. This was part of his conditioning on Bay Street, it appeared: deflect emotion and focus on the facts in front of you. "We filed the separation papers yesterday. The house will be going up for sale shortly. Joint custody of Paul. No alimony!"

"You sound relieved."

"Relieved? I'm ecstatic." His voice did not sound ecstatic.

"That's good to know. Usually, these things are devastating. You don't seem too bothered by the disruption."

"It's like paying off a bad debt, Dad. Trust me, it's only going to be upwards and onwards from here. By the way, we started the IPO project." Damian's voice got animated only on the last statement.

"I heard."

"From your friends at the old firm? Maybe I should pick your brain."

"I'm keeping my sources confidential on this one. You'll have to do your own digging. Have you thought of your son in all this?"

"He's a kid. He'll bounce back."

"You and Sylvana have demanding jobs. So, let me ask you, when you each have him in your separate custody, will you be able to spend quality time with him?"

"We'll figure it out. Let it happen first."

"You rarely spend time with him now. It'll get harder when you're on your own. When other relationships enter the equation." He envied his son. Damian could start again, he couldn't.

"We'll figure it out." Then, Damian seemed to cotton on to the opening he was being given. "Do you want to fill in the hole from time to time?"

"I'm not averse to spending time with Paul. But it will only be on a contingency basis. He is *your* son. *You* will be responsible for the values he carries into adulthood."

"I got it. You never let me forget it while growing up."

And I must have failed miserably. "I'll be in touch." Avery hung up, unconvinced that he had achieved anything. Damian was a shallow human being, and he did not know where his son had inherited this trait from.

***

There were the nights when he awoke believing the ground had opened up beneath him and that he had nothing to hold onto. And the dreams, of running to catch a train, but it was always leaving the station ahead of him. Those dreams were less frequent now than shortly after he had lost his job; then they had ebbed, only to come roaring back after Pat passed away, rendering him incapable of functioning for days on end. The company had offered out-placement counselling when he had been made redundant, but that had only been whitewash over the loss of a way of life.

He remembered the day he had been visited in his office by Samuels and Brock; it was the day that Pat had received her last dose of chemo and was spaced out at home. Avery had advised his administrative assistant that he would be coming in late to the office, after accompanying Pat to the hospital and back and settling her on the couch at home in front of the TV. When he arrived at Sand around 11 a.m., the President and COO were already seated in his office. They weren't smiling or chatting. They were sitting there, waiting.

"Hello, gentlemen. To what do I owe the privilege? Sorry, I am a bit late today. I had to take Pat for her last treatment. The nurses sang her a song to celebrate her finishing her treatments successfully."

Samuels leaned back in the visitor chair, a sad smile on his face. "Sorry to hear about your troubles in these last few months."

Avery took his jacket off and hung it on the peg behind the doors. "What can I do for you today? This *is* an unexpected visit."

"Shut the door while you're at it," Samuels said, and his voice had taken on a harshness.

Avery complied and returned to his seat, facing them, his palms turning clammy.

Samuels exchanged a glance with Brock and leaned across the desk. "We'll make this quick, Avery. I am terminating your employment with Sand as of today."

Avery blinked.

"I know this is sudden. But that is how it is usually, and it's best that way. Of course, there will be a generous settlement. Olga will come in shortly with the details."

Avery managed to find his voice. "But, why? Am I allowed to ask why?"

"Divergent visions of the company's future direction. Let's just call it that."

"But I did support the launch of Depo-Gen."

"You went through the motions." Brock spoke up for the first time and the nasal tone of his voice was annoying. "Your heart wasn't in it."

"My heart was with my sick wife."

Unruffled, Brock rattled off a list as if he had memorized it. "You missed launch meetings, were late with press releases, did not show up for the press conference—"

Avery interrupted him. "I said, I was caring for a sick wife. I couldn't be present in person at key events. But they took place without a hitch, nevertheless, and my team carried the launch through as planned."

Samuels laid a hand on Brock, cutting him off. "Martin, we don't need the list at this time. Avery, there comes a time when ways do part, even between the best partners. We could go on for hours justifying our respective positions, and that would be futile." He rose, and Brock rose with him. "Olga will come in now and go over the details. Best of luck. And give my regards to Pat."

They did not shake his hand but left the office immediately. Seconds later, Olga made her entrance.

***

On the Friday, he started sorting through old albums. If he was going to downsize, he'd better get rid of clutter. He lingered over the ones from his childhood. Black-and-white photos of a toothy kid in an open field in Scarborough (now converted into a sprawling residential subdivision); Heidi, his mother, who stayed home to raise him: an apron and a headscarf were signature items of her domestic attire; his father, Helmut, an ambulance driver in Germany, then after eight years of working dead-end jobs in auto-repair shops in Canada, standing proud in his Toyota Canada uniform when the division was founded in 1964. A picture of his mother and father at a dance in the sixties, suited and elegant—hard to tell that they, when newly married, had been incarcerated in Birkenau during the tail end of the Second World War; their crime: Heidi was a Jew whose family went back four generations in Germany. In the picture, their dance seemed to signify gratitude towards each other, defiance towards oppression, and hope for the life in their new homeland of Canada where they were among the few from that dreaded death camp to enjoy a second chance. Now he understood why his father had built that first cottage out in the boonies. To average Canadians a cottage was a refuge from the drudgery of the city, to Helmut Mann it was in case those Nazi devils came back.

A second album brought tears to his eyes—his life with Pat. High school sweethearts. He remembered the graduation dances, the Valentine's Day drives in his old Ford Mustang down to the Beaches, and sometimes further afield to Cobourg Beach, where they would hold hands, dream about the future, and be anonymous. Their wedding pictures, when film had turned to colour, though faded now: running under a shower of flowers thrown by family and friends; Heidi all dressed up, wearing a hat, but confined to a wheelchair after the stroke that had felled her the previous year; the car with the tin cans trailing behind them, Niagara Falls in the background where they honeymooned. Later pictures when Damian came on the scene, and Avery was by then a young executive at Sand Pharmaceuticals. His son had always been dressed in brand-name clothes, as they had never intended him to be found wanting among his peers—that was where they had gone wrong. He shut the album, for although the pictures were of happy times, they were of times past.

The picture that wasn't in the album was the one frozen in his mind, of Pat on her final stretch at the palliative care unit in 2008, as the financial world was collapsing around them. He remembered the day well, for Lehmann Brothers had declared bankruptcy that morning—it was repeating on the overhead TV monitor above her bed. She was wraithlike, and the look of death had been emerging for some weeks: the protruding lower jaw, the drawn eyes, the creeping pallor, the draining of life from one day to the next.

"I'm sorry, darling," she whispered, waking up in the late evening as he dozed on the visitor's couch next to her bed.

He rubbed his eyes. "Sorry? For what?"

"For leaving you with this mess to sort out." Her voice was sharper than usual.

"I'm not in any mess. I've got a generous settlement that will run for a few years. There's money in the bank. You have to focus on getting yourself well." He knew he sounded fake.

"I'm not getting well this time. The family…Damian…is so unsettled. The banks are going bankrupt. And you're still mourning your departure from Sand. I wish I could help you. You mustn't mourn me."

He rose from the couch and took her cold, bony hand. There were no words to be spoken. He didn't want to sound fake anymore, silence was preferred. A tear rolled down his cheek and fell on hers where it fused with a droplet flowing out of her eye. Mingling together, the larger rivulet ran off her face to be absorbed in the pillow. That picture was indelible and didn't need a camera to remain in his mind forever.

Now, he took the albums down to the basement and left them beside the boxes of Pat's clothes.

***

On the Saturday afternoon, he dressed in a suit and chose a red tie. He had plenty of suits—and ties— from the old days, clothes he didn't have an opportunity to wear anymore. He decided he would buy a bottle of wine from the vintage collection at the liquor store, and also a bouquet of flowers for Sarah as the party was being held at her home. He steeled himself for meeting a lot of people, something he was not accustomed to of late—in particular, people who would be forming impressions of him.

Sarah's house was in Willowdale, a quiet subdivision off the main drag of Yonge Street, with stately bungalows, many modernized into two- and three-storey mansions in the last decade. Hers was a renovated two-storey with a brick and stucco facade and ornate, glass- panelled double doors. After all, this was a former judge's residence, he reminded himself. Avery could have afforded to buy a house here as his career grew, to cash-in on a larger real-estate price gain, but he had opted to remain in his modest bungalow in Scarborough because it provided stability to Damian and Pat—in retrospect, stability was just another form of vapourware.

The front door was unlocked, with a "Welcome to Our Party" sign, and yet he rang the bell before stepping in. There was an immediate rise in the noise level, and organized chaos reigned inside. Children were running around; toys, books, party streamers, and balloons competed for attention amidst adults who stood in clumps around a dining table filled with finger food, cake, and pastries. A bar off to the side, with another bunch of adults hanging around, was arrayed with a range of alcoholic and non-alcoholic beverages. A bearded man behind the bar, wearing a sweatshirt proclaiming "Proud to be Thirty-Five," was serving drinks, sloshing most of his efforts over the counter and onto the faux-wooden floor.

Sarah emerged, wearing a yellow party hat; her face looked flushed and happy. "Avery! Welcome. Ooh, flowers! Not sure Brian goes for flowers. But he'll take the wine."

"The flowers are for you."

She looked surprised, then a grateful smile broke through. "Can't remember the last time a man gave me flowers. Thanks! Come in and meet the family." She grabbed his hand like an excited teenager and dragged him into the melee.

And he met the family. Sarah took him to the nearest relative around, Emily, the associate professor, who was neatly buttering a scone beside the food table.

"Start with Emily, I'm sure she doesn't bite," Sarah said, as Emily bit into her scone. Then Sarah skipped away to the kitchen to put the flowers in water.

"Oh, you look like an Avery," Emily said, licking her fingers delicately.

"My emails must wear my personality on their sleeves," he said.

"They do. Remarkably frank. Most men in the dating game are not. Glad you could come today."

Emily was bespectacled, dark-haired like her mother, and slim. She turned out to be edgily erudite, unapologetic for having read his emails, and well versed in contemporary affairs, from the upcoming election to corporate corruption. After flitting around various topics, they returned to the election. *She's gauged my breadth, now she's going for depth.*

"Glad we're on the same team," he said, after he had cautiously established her party affiliation.

"None of the parties are delivering on their promises, but the Centrists are the best of the bad lot," Emily said dismissively, picking up a piece of cheese and placing it carefully on a cracker.

"Politics is about convincing a bunch of average people to give a smarter person, or persons, a mandate so that they can do what they want for the next four years. Our job is to pick the right people and hope that hubris does not turn them."

"That's like expecting David to keep slaying more Goliaths. He ended up seducing Bathsheba and murdering her husband Uriah."

"You know your Biblical history?"

"Mom read to us a lot. I owe her for nudging me into my present career. I wanted to be a lawyer like my father. Then she took me into court one day and we sat in the public area while Dad was passing sentence on a man who had sexually assaulted a teenager. The look of pure evil on the accused man's face, directed towards my father, convinced me that I was not cut out for the law. I think Mom orchestrated that visit."

Avery was beginning to lose his initial embarrassment and get comfortable with Emily and her frankness. Then she was rudely dragged away by a guest to another part of the room. *So much for house parties enabling deep discussions: they are no better than networking events where all we do is exchange business cards.*

Emily's husband, Ethan, a recently graduated doctor doing a residency at the Toronto General, was quiet-spoken and more concerned with herding their children, Brittany and Jacob, away from the sweets on the main table. "Speeds them up," he offered, "and then we diagnose them with fancy acronyms: ADHD, ELD, ASD, and so on."

Paula, Brian's wife, was a stay-at-home mom, having put a RN career on hold to care for her two children, Megan and Miles. She was more concerned with how they were outgrowing clothing sizes, and she was deliberating whether shopping for clothes online was a better option than commuting into the Eaton Centre on a regular basis. She excused herself when Miles spilled his drink and had to be taken away for a change of clothes. At that point, Avery decided to get a drink himself and walked up to the bar.

"You must be Brian," he said to the bartender who was happily advertising his age. "Happy birthday! I'm Avery."

"Oh, you're Mom's friend." The bearded man imparted a wide smile. "What are you drinking?"

"A beer for now."

"Coming up," and more froth spilled on the counter before the tankard reached Avery. Brian came across as a chubby, cheerful, and inept football fan, but his eyes had a sharpness that betrayed an agile mind, like his sister's. Since most of the hangers-on at the bar had drifted to other parts of the house, Avery decided to stay and chat. "Nice of your mother to give you a party."

"Yes. I get so busy I don't remember my own birthday."

Sarah sailed by with more pastries on a tray. "Hope you're having a good time, Avery? Brian, you might want to pick Avery's brain. He used to be a big honcho at Sand."

"Really?"

Avery nodded. "Thirty years. Before the inevitable putting out to pasture."

"And he can't seem to let go," Sarah said. "Brian might give you some reasons for wanting to leave it all behind." And with that mysterious comment, she headed off to re-stock the food table.

An embarrassed silence descended. Brian broke the logjam. "I'm representing some clients in a suit against Sand. Hope that doesn't make you uncomfortable."

"The cancer connection with Depo-Med?"

"You're well informed."

"Well, I know as much as anyone on the street. This cancer scare came after my time at the firm. I don't think it will have any legs, though. Depo-Med has been on the market for a long time, and its clinical trials were exhaustive."

"It's not with Depo-Med itself, but with its generic version."

A couple of loud guests, a bit inebriated, came over and interrupted their conversation, looking for refills. Brian apologized with, "We'll have to carry on this conversation later," and turned to serve his guests.

Avery moved over to the far end of the room, his brows furrowed. Through an open door, he could see into the adjoining room, which looked like a library, filled with a grand piano and large bookcases lining the walls. Sarah had seated the children—her grandchildren and others belonging to adult guests—in a circle on a large Persian rug. She had an illustrated story book in her hands. "No party is complete without story time," she announced, hushing the unruly bunch. Then she launched into "The Ass in the Lion's Skin" from Aesop's Fables. Her absorption in the tale was infectious, for the kids, who had been busily romping about the house only minutes earlier, settled forward with elbows cradling chins or hands moving others out of the way to get a better glimpse of the story-teller. A pang shot through Avery as he watched the tableau. He would have given anything to see Paul among this group of children. Although Paul was older, his grandson would have benefited enormously by receiving a story in the way it was meant to be delivered: animated, imbued with sparkle and excitement, with side explanations of the metaphors and symbols contained within, lessons that were relevant today despite the story's age, and with the fullness of the story conveyed by a caring human being, all in a way that an iPad could never provide despite all its technological versatility.

He moved away from his observations and went out onto the patio. The blast of cold air was invigorating after the warmth and human bustle inside. And then the other remark that Brian had made returned. *It's not with Depo-Med itself, but with its generic version.*

The scene that day with Pat, five years before she was first diagnosed, returned. He had come home after work one evening to see a bunch of prescriptions on the dining room table.

"Hi, Honey! I'm home!"

"Dinner will be ready in ten minutes," she called from the kitchen.

"You've been to the pharmacy, I see. Did you fill my cholesterol prescription too?" He tossed his jacket on the chair and went over to the liquor cabinet to fix himself a pre-dinner drink.

The stove's exhaust fan had come on. She must have not heard him.

He returned to the dining table with his glass of scotch and water and rifled through the prescriptions. He did not see his Lipitor, but there were a couple of prescriptions that he did not recognize the pharmaceutical name for, although one in particular made him open his eyes wide. Puzzled, he went into the kitchen with the new packets clutched in his hands.

Pat was taking a pot roast out of the oven. The smell of garlic and herbs instantly made his mouth water.

He tossed the packets on the kitchen counter. "What's with this?"

"Isn't it great?" she said over her shoulder, checking the tenderness of the meat. "Our insurance company is now insisting on generics as a first option for a hundred percent coverage. The brand names have dropped to eighty percent coverage. So, I bought the generics where they were available. Your Lipitor is called Atovarstatin and my estrogen is now called Estrofem."

"But you've also bought Depo-Gen instead of Depo-Med. It's the generic version of what you've been taking all along."

"Isn't that good? Supporting a similar product from your company? The pharmacist said it's just come on the market. And you didn't tell me." She interrupted what she was doing and looked wide-eyed at him, and he swore under his breath for not letting her into the tussles he'd had over the generics invasion at Sand. But Pat was of a different ilk, too gentle and hopeful about the world to understand the forces of greed and power that lurked within it, and he had sheltered her from the murkier issues at the firm. And yet, her unwitting purchase of Depo-Gen felt like the ultimate betrayal to him.

He shrugged and scooped up the prescriptions. "I guess so," he replied, returning to the dining room and throwing the packs back on the table. The last he remembered of that incident was picking up his scotch, draining the glass, and saying, "Thanks for getting me my Lipitor, or Apova...whatever...statin you call it."

"Penny for your thoughts?"

He swung around and Emily had come out onto the patio.

"I was recalling happier times when I had a family," he said, struggling to find the right words.

"And you don't have one now?"

"I was an only child. My parents are dead. My wife is dead and my only son is going through a divorce. I'll never be able to match that crowd inside."

"One can be 'alone in a crowd.'"

"Hemingway?"

"No. My mother. She tries to embrace people and be in the centre of things. But I know that she's alone. Has been ever since Dad died."

"I'm convinced now that everyone is alone. We are born alone and die alone and between those bookends we meet a few people."

"But those people can enrich your lonely journey. Make you a richer person upon arrival. Wherever you arrive."

Her brown eyes were surveying him closely. He nodded. "You have a point there. I built a cabin in the woods for myself. To end my days alone, like we were intended to."

He saw the disappointment in her face. "Oh, how boring."

A loud round of clapping rose from the slightly cracked-open patio door.

"They'll be cutting the cake soon. We'd better go inside," Emily said, extending her hand as if to lead him inside like a child.

Here he was trying to break away from it all, and at each attempt, someone was reaching out to pull him back in.

"Okay, let's go inside and sing 'Happy Birthday!'" he said and followed her indoors.

Brian was making a speech with a cake-coated knife in his hand. "I want to thank you all for coming today. And I want to thank my mom for organizing everything. It's like I never left home. She always celebrates my birthday."

There was backslapping and cheering, streamers flew across the room, and Sarah emerged from the kitchen again with Brian's generous slices now reposing on a large tray for serving to guests.

Today was not the day to have that deeper discussion on Sand with Brian. *Let him have his party.* But Avery made a mental note that he would contact Brian soon.

When he left that evening, Sarah saw him to the door. "Thanks for coming. I'm sorry I couldn't spend too much time with you today."

"Don't worry, I had much to amuse myself with. I listened in on your story session too."

"You did? That's a tradition in our family. I always read to Brian and Emily when they were children."

"You have a wonderful family. Thanks for inviting me."

"I hope you'll come again."

"I will." This time it was his turn to peck her on the cheek. He let his lips stay awhile and she did not withdraw.

"Goodnight, Avery."

***

When he got home, it was dark. He fixed himself a scotch and water, put on a CD from his Mantovani Classics collection, and sat on his recliner by the window. This was a perch where he had spent many evenings after Pat had passed away. And yet today, he had seen another side of life. A real life with its imperfections and joys. A side that he could belong to again. A side that would be deliciously experiential while it lasted and devastatingly lonely when it ended, for surely it too would end, like all good things. Was it easier to not enter, but to run away and hide out in that cottage by the lake? He was gripped by a sense of unknowing. He downed his drink. Another drink would clarify the picture further, make sleep easier.

Across the street, a light was on in the living room of Stan Barclay's house. Through the open blinds Avery could see his friend sitting on the couch, reading some papers. Stan rose and paced, then returned to his papers. His step did not exhibit the optimism he projected at his political rallies; this was the pacing of a worried man. *Maybe we are all different when we are alone, more authentic. Maybe I'll be more real when I head off to my cottage. Maybe Sarah is simply a nice episode, and should remain so.*

Avery rose and went to pour himself another drink.

Chapter 9

The old man licked the flap of the envelope and sealed it. This letter had taken him three months to write, with many drafts, many sections added and then taken out; there had been multiple sources that had to be checked and re-checked before he was satisfied with the end result. He stuck a stamp on the envelope. This had to be done in the old-fashioned way. He did not trust email for such a sensitive document. His Yahoo account had been hacked recently, and today he was being impersonated by hackers marketing Viagra, costume jewellery, and software to *his contacts,* including the recipient of this letter. How could the addressee trust an email with such a story coming from him now? It would be automatically relegated as an extension of those Nigerian 419ers with their tales of being stranded without money in exotic locales.

He walked down to the crossroad. Today was the first day of May—Labour Day in the old country, or as the Nazis had renamed it, "The Day of National Work," with parades and speeches and celebrations commemorating the ascent of the working class to their due place in society. Over here in North America, this was another normal day, because Labour Day had been conveniently moved to the end of summer, and the return to school and work. And the working class was steadily shrinking as jobs were being outsourced to the Third World, where a new middle class was emerging.

Going downhill was getting as difficult as the uphill climb, and he leaned heavily on the walking stick that he used for these excursions. For a while now he had been wondering whether it was time to put up the "For Sale" sign and move back east into a retirement home. Today that desire was stronger. The proceeds on the sale of this property plus his pension should keep him comfortably off until he died. Should he take one more trip back to Germany, to revisit his past and put some space between him and Canada for when the yoghurt hit the fan, as it surely must when this letter reached its destination? He'd be a sitting duck up here when the hordes of paparazzi and journalists descended on him like swarms from his hives, only they would beat him up for information until he caved in, and he was not sure he had sufficient reserves of energy in him to withstand their persistence.

Maybe he should toss the letter in the trash and return to his bees and enjoy them for as long as he could. But his feet kept heading downhill, and very soon he was at the general store, which had a post office outlet at the rear.

"Good morning!" Bob, the storekeeper, called out from behind the cash counter. "You're up early today. Milk's arrived, so has the newspaper."

"I watched the ferry coming in. I was up at three o'clock."

"Oh-oh. You haven't been sleeping much lately? I've seen your house lights on across the way when I shut down for the night."

"I've been writing. Telling a story."

"What, your autobiography? A novel?"

"A letter."

Leaving Bob frowning, he went to the back where Bob's wife, Lydia, was busy stacking parcels.

"Be right with you, Mr. Smith. Didn't expect any customers this early." She hefted a pile of bulky mail packages and took them into the back room. Smith took out his envelope and laid it carefully on the postal counter.

"Do you want that express delivery—guaranteed three-day service?" she asked, returning and adjusting her glasses.

"Three days, eh? Okay. You don't have anything faster?"

"I can do express courier, next day delivery, but it will cost you three times more."

"Okay, I'll do the three-day thing."

She processed the envelope and dropped it into a box beside her. He leaned over the counter. "You are sure it's safe, *ja?*"

She giggled. "What, you've got gold in it?"

He grinned. "Drugs." He couldn't resist the irony.

"Oh, then we surely have to confiscate it."

He liked this banter with Lydia. She and Bob were the only souls who talked to him or entered his domain. Lydia did his housecleaning once every two weeks and Bob helped him with maintaining the grounds of his property. He trusted Lydia and Bob.

"And I'll buy some eggs today, and some bacon. And my newspaper of course. I think I have enough milk."

"Bread?"

"Oh, yes, nearly forgot. You know my kind, yeast-free."

"Bavaria's best, coming up."

She moved from the postal counter into the store, fetched him the items he needed, and brought them up to the cash register.

"Thank you, dear. Now you know why I don't shop in the big supermarket. Oh, before I forget…" He dug into his jacket pocket and pulled out a jar with a ribbon around it. "I got you something. From my reserve collection. This is for you and Bob, and not for sale."

Lydia took the jar of honey from him with an excited peal of laughter. "Oh, thank you. This will go wonderfully with our morning tea. I hope you'll be giving us a fresh supply this fall for sale. People drive up all the way from Nanaimo to buy your honey, you know."

The old man sighed. "Unfortunately, there will be no honey from me this year. I'm getting a little tired."

Lydia looked at him with a worried frown. Then she shrugged and regained her composure. "There I go, seeking profit all the time. I agree, you're entitled to a break." She looked down at his groceries. "This is too much for you to haul. I think I'm going to run you up the hill in the truck." She looked at Bob, who nodded.

"Oh, that's wonderful. I was dreading the climb back."

Sitting in the cab in Lydia's truck he watched the water reappear over the hill as they took the two-minute ride back up to his house. She was silent, probably digesting the fact that after ten years, there would be no honey for sale at the store, the sole distribution outlet for Hank's Harmonious Honey, a name Lydia had come up with and a key differentiating factor of their small-business enterprise from other convenience stores in the area. Suddenly, a sadness overcame him. This was probably going to be the last time he would interact with these people and their store in the usual way. He had reached his decision while walking downhill to the store. When she pulled up to his door, he disembarked stiffly, came around the truck, and gave Lydia a big hug.

"Thank you, my dear. Thank you for all the help over the years."

She blushed, as if surprised by this outpouring from her client. "Well, Mr. Smith, I was wondering when you were going to show some emotion. It's a pleasure working for you. Everything so organized and punctual with you, unlike with some of my other clients." Then she peered into his face. "Is everything all right?"

"Yes, for now. But tomorrow is another day."

"You're missing Bruno, aren't you? We could get you another dog, you know."

"I have no more energy for dogs now. Besides I don't want Bruno...ah...replaced. He was irreplaceable."

She blushed again. "Sorry, I didn't mean it that way."

"I know you didn't. Thank you for the ride."

"You will call if you need help, won't you?"

"I will." He waved as she drove away. By the look on her face, he suspected she wasn't quite convinced that everything was indeed okay. He was sure that she and Bob would have a new item for discussion around their dinner table tonight, in addition to the usual local gossip and the minutia of running a general store on an island.

After a hearty breakfast—the bacon had been an extra for him today as he had felt like celebrating, having completed his mission—he went out into the garden and walked among the white boxes, hearing the muffled buzzing going on inside. He wouldn't add the second level of super boxes this year, he wouldn't need to, for the bees would be leaving early. The honey house, located at the other end of the line of boxes, a wooden work shack that housed the storage jars and the extractor for releasing honey from the frames, stood padlocked—it wouldn't see much activity from him this year either. He turned his attention to the boxes of hives and ran his hand gently along one. "My dearies, soon I will set you free for the last time. Please travel far and wide and continue to help the earth as you were meant to."

He returned to the house, picked up the real-estate section of the newspaper, and marked off a couple of realtors who might list his property. He called a travel agency and booked a flight to Berlin for the night of July 1. All that was needed to be done could be done in eight weeks. If they needed him, they had eight weeks.

The he sat back in his armchair to read the rest of the newspaper. The headline in the main section caught his eye: "Federal candidates make final campaign stops before election tomorrow."

He didn't think he would vote this year. He didn't trust any of the candidates.

Chapter 10

The writ dropped at the end of March, and life got very busy after that for Avery. He barely had time to keep in touch with Sarah. This was totally complicit on his part, for he needed time and distance to consider his relationship with her. When Stan requested him to assist in the campaign office, he didn't refuse. When he was co-opted into the lawn-sign distribution brigade, he didn't refuse. When he was asked to field the phone lines two evenings a week to call people for campaign contributions, he didn't refuse.

When he asked himself why he was doing this, when he had only agreed to drive seniors to the polling booth, he realized that seeing his neighbour's worried look that night had all to do with it. He could not let Stan fail this time. It was as if he would fail again too. He had failed once when he had been turfed out of his company in the most inglorious manner, and he had failed again when he lost Pat to the cancer that may have been caused by a drug that he had been unable to prevent her from taking; this election was his third strike, just as it was for Stan. He couldn't let himself, or Stan, miss this pitch. The challenge, once thrown, was one he couldn't resist. He was vicariously invested in Stan, and in winning.

A campaign bus pulled up opposite Stan's house daily during the campaign, in the early morning and late in the evening, ferrying Stan and his support team on the voter trail. Avery attended a couple of the local rallies and observed that Stan's powerful oratory hadn't lost its edge. He was a commanding figure on the podium: sweat streaming off his balding head, repeating his slogan, "Change Is in the Air," over and over as if it were a reggae refrain; he got crowds on their feet, rocking to a Bob Marley beat. Avery rode the campaign bus back with him on the first occasion after a rally at a public school. Following a forty-five-minute speech and plenty of roaring and cheering from the audience, Stan lay collapsed on the back seat of the bus on the way home, a wet towel over his head.

"You'll get wiped out before election day, Stanley," Lizzy was saying as she fussed about him, amidst a bunch of sycophantic teen supporters who were also on board, waving flags through the windows.

"It gives me energy, Lizzy," he said, waving her away. "Go get those kids something to drink. Dey going a bit hoarse and all."

Avery sidled up to the seat Lizzy vacated as she went to look after the young supporters. Suddenly, a steely but cold hand gripped him, and Stan removed the cold compress from over his eyes. "I'm glad what you doing for me, my friend. We gonna do this dis time. I can feel it in my blood. After all those tries in de past."

"It ain't over until it's over, they say, Stan. Bernard Phelps has got more lawn signs up than you. I counted them."

"Lawn signs are not votes, my friend."

"You've got to hit the seniors centres a bit more. They have shorter memories than the kids."

"I'm leaving dem for the end of de campaign so my visits will be fresh in their minds."

"We are already in Week Four. I wouldn't leave it much longer."

Stan seemed to have acted on the advice, for three days later, Avery received his email bulletin from the Sixty-Five Plus Club, and it announced that Stanley Barclay would be the keynote speaker at a regional meeting of all the clubs in the eastern GTA, which was being convened at a banquet hall in the riding.

Avery drove to the event. The hall was packed with over three hundred people in the audience. The older members were in front and they had come early to reserve their seats. There were lots of walkers and canes and louder than normal conversation. A table overflowed with sandwiches and coffee, and people were milling around—free food went down well at these events, it appeared. Avery took his seat at the back of the room and watched Stan and his entourage enter, shaking hands, making their way slowly down the centre aisle, along with officials of the Sixty-Five Plus Club, towards their seats on the stage at the far end.

The regional president rose to speak, and it took a full five minutes before everyone resumed their places, stopped clinking cutlery, and started to pay attention to the speaker. Avery only heard the man's concluding words before he introduced Stan. ". . . and we are honoured today to have Mr. Stanley Barclay as our speaker. Mr. Barclay, as you know, has lived in our community for over thirty years. He is a local businessman, and we have all enjoyed his tasty cuisine over the years. . ." The lights in the room surged bright and dipped and there was flash by the sound amplifier. The microphone went dead. People at the head table stared nervously at each other. The house lights remained on, so this was not a general power failure—perhaps a power surge, but one that had knocked out the audio equipment. The sound technician kept fiddling with his control board and scratching his head.

Stan immediately stood up, came around the head table and stepped towards the audience with his hands raised for silence. "Ladies and gentlemen, we may have minor setbacks from time to time, but we must continue our mission. When I was growing up in the islands, we didn't have electricity. So, if you will stay and pay attention, I will speak without a microphone."

His voice carried to the end of the room, but Avery wondered how many hearing-impaired seniors would have been able to hear him above the rumble of conversation that had started to creep in with the silencing of the microphone. The sound guy was shaking his head and throwing up his hands.

Stan launched into his oratory.

"Ladies and gentlemen, over the last five years we have seen the lifestyle of seniors steadily erode. Social benefits have been steadily shrinking, Old Age Security is being clawed back, and several medical procedures are being excluded from provincial plans. Those living in poverty have increased and many of them are people like you—seniors."

Some nods went on in the front rows. But people closer to Avery at the back shouted, "Speak louder, we can't hear you!" A couple in the row ahead of Avery rose, grabbed their coats, and started to leave. The sound guy was fiddling with his equipment.

Stan went into higher pitch, but Avery detected a hoarseness in his voice. *He will not last much longer with this crowd.*

"…we will fight to restore your privileges, restore dignity in your sunset years. For you have earned it." More nods in the front rows, a few cheers, but mostly mumbling in the rest of the room. The mumbling was overtaking Stan's voice, and soon, even Avery was unable to hear him. But Stan kept up, waving his hands, swaying his hips, a vein bulging in his temple, sweat streaming down his face. Finally, all Avery could see was this fiercely gesticulating caricature on stage while the audience went about its own agenda.

Then with a crack and a ripple the microphone went live and Stan's voice blasted everyone into wakefulness. "I want to thank you all for inviting me today." Stan was wrapping up, and he looked at the sound engineer helplessly, as if to say "Do you expect me to repeat my spiel all over again, you idiot?" A roar of applause went through the room but Avery felt the audience was clapping for the soundman and not for the speaker.

The regional president quickly grabbed the podium and went into a stream of thanks to everyone who had helped organize the event. Stan returned to his seat, shoulders hunched, wiping his face with a handkerchief.

Avery decided it was time to leave.

***

Martin Brock chose the indigo tie and navy-blue pinstriped suit for his visit to Dr. Bernard Phelps. His wardrobe was lined with suits and ties of every hue, a procurement pastime he had indulged in heavily after his third wife had been replaced with online dating. Some suits reminded him of conquest, others of disappointment. Today's suit was one that he had worn on the night he had successfully seduced a corporate executive from his advertising agency; he was her business client, and she couldn't refuse him a few extras. He had enjoyed great sex with her over the next four months, and then gently let her down before going on his next foray. He was sure that she must have been relieved to go back to "business as usual."

His SUV slid quietly along the fifteen-minute ride down Queen Street to the Beaches, to the headquarters of the incumbent right-wing MP running for re-election. He flicked radio stations to one that played Contemporary Rock, and hummed under his breath. The world was good, with only the occasional cloud, like the one that hovered in front of him as he drove. He hoped that it would soon clear away.

Phelps's campaign office was buzzing. A bank of computers was arranged in a circle in the middle of the large converted warehouse. A dozen operators were talking on headsets as they typed. Brock wondered whether there were that many constituents in the riding to warrant this kind of a phone assault.

Phelps, a large, red-headed man in his late fifties, wearing a blue golf shirt and khaki pants, reminded Brock of the last time they had played eighteen holes at Angus Glen together—too long ago. They had to get another round into the calendar soon. And he had to make sure that Phelps won, again. The MP, seeing Brock enter, left a group of eager interns and came over, extending a large, soft hand that tightened into a vise on contact.

"Welcome, Martin! You've brought in the action today, it seems. Our telemarketers are in full swing."

"Thought I'd check out the battlefront. I also brought a little contribution." Brock pulled out the envelope from his jacket pocket and waved it in the air.

"Ah, thank you! Let me bring you over to our secretary here, who will receipt it." Phelps winked, then raised his voice. "All contributions go to the electoral officer who distributes it to the political parties. Got to keep this above board, you know."

After the paperwork was completed by a flustered, middle-aged volunteer secretary, Phelps took Brock over to the telemarketing pod. From the overheard conversations, Brock understood why so many were manning the phones.

"You're calling non-party members too?"

"We are calling everyone who lives in the riding. The party faithful are locked in. We need the undecided vote and we need to steal a few weak Centrist and Leftist supporters. Our intelligence gives us a pretty good idea of who they are."

"That kid over there is offering a Centrist supporter a ride to the polling station."

Phelps smiled. "Stan Barclay had a disastrous showing at the Sixty-Five Plus meeting yesterday. We're calling in to assure their members of a stronger alternative to Stan."

After they had passed the telemarketers, Martin lowered his voice. "Are you on track for the health portfolio?"

"That's what I'm told. And I haven't yet fallen foul of the party hierarchy."

"I may need your help with this rumour that's been circulating about one of our generic drugs."

"Yes. I've been reading about it. It's troubling. How come we missed it? I was on your board at the time."

"You know it's not true."

"Well, that's what you're going to have to stick with."

"I think we have it in hand. But I thought I would warn you should things get out of control."

"Thanks. In the meantime, I'll see what I can do to quell any questions that arise within the party. What's your plan B?"

"A few more people might have to die."

Phelps raised his eyebrows and lowered his voice to a pitch below Brock's. "Well, I hope it doesn't come to that. But a plan B is a good thing. Call me if you need any help. Even those kids over there have a plan B on how to get Centrist seniors out to the voting stations."

Later, when Brock got into his SUV, the clouds had dissipated to offer a break of sun, and he felt relieved. The visit to Phelps had been rewarding. He figured he'd clock off early today and head to the club. A round of golf, despite the cold weather, and some drinks with the regulars would help conclusively in quelling his misgivings. And then there was that blond real-estate woman who had returned his query on the dating site this morning…a promising evening ahead. He had plenty of time to deliberate on Phelps's words, "Call me if you need any help."

Chapter 11

" "Winning this one is important to you, isn't it?" Sarah asked as she played with the olive in her martini. Avery was glad for the soft lighting that masked his features. They were in Caesar's, an Italian family restaurant with a quiet section, away from the raucous gatherings in the main dining room. This was the night before the election and Avery had decided he couldn't stand the tension anymore. Sarah had gladly consented to a dinner date, their first.

"Stan deserves to win. Besides, big business has been steadily infiltrating government for too long."

She peered directly at him, pointing the cocktail stick like a little sabre. "But you need a win too."

He shrugged. He was cornered. "I've had too many losses in recent times."

"It depends on what you consider a loss versus a lesson. Barry's passing taught me that solitude is our lot."

Avery studied the menu. "I think I will have the steak—well done." His nervousness was giving him an urge to either gorge on food, have sex, or get drunk—maybe those infernal pills were having a long-tail residual effect. He knew he couldn't spoil things with a wrong move at this stage of their emerging relationship.

"The salmon for me," she added without another glance at the menu.

They talked about their grandchildren over dinner, avoiding the election, or rather, she artfully got him off the topic that was gnawing at him. He tried not to drink too much wine, but with every sip he took she began to look more desirable to him. There was a lot to talk about when it came to grandchildren, at least for Sarah. The two older girls, Megan and Brittany, were in school now and into ballet and music; the boys, Jacob and Miles, were toddlers, curiously pulling things off shelves to explore them, experimenting with a few days in the week at daycare to improve their social skills, and beginning to give their parents—and grandmother when she had them over for sleepovers—the chance of a good night's sleep. She made the subject of grandchildren interesting, and Avery forgot his doubts and conflicted emotions as she spoke and he listened. But after a while, he returned to the election.

"I wish Stan had done more work with the seniors," he said.

She sighed. "Well, he's only human. He did what he could."

"I'm pretty damned sure the technician who blew the microphone at the Sixty-Five Plus Club was on the payroll of the other guys. I wish I could prove it, though."

She sighed again. "It won't do you any good now."

He continued to analyze the weak points of Stan's campaign until coffee arrived.

"Tell me more about your grandson," she said, pouring milk into her coffee. "You don't say much about him."

"Your grandchildren absorb you so much, I didn't want to throw him into the mix. Don't worry about it."

"I would like to know more. Honestly."

Avery sighed. "Paul's not in a good space right now with his parents going through a messy divorce. They were barricaded on either side of their house, duking it out over the spoils of their marriage for months before they tired and settled. The kid witnessed every taunt, curse, and barb they lobbed at each other, including the odd blow."

"Do you spend time with him?" She was studying him closely.

"When I get the chance. He prefers his iPad to humans. I wish he would read."

"Why don't you bring him to the bookshop? We have a large children's books section, as you know. And he can be a part of the computerization of that section, as I've decided to take your advice, rent out the top floor, and concentrate on downstairs."

A mix of euphoria and excitement swept through him. "You mean, my advice has benefited someone?"

She smiled and reached out to take his hand. "Heroes are not always politicians. Sometimes they are everyday people, Avery."

He laughed. "They used to call me Everyman in school—my name didn't help."

She blushed, then laughed too. "I didn't think of it like that. But yes— why not? Avery... Mann!"

"I wonder if Paul will actually like the bookshop. I don't want to disappoint you if he turns around and utters his favourite words: 'I'm bored.'"

"Well, all you can do is try. Let me know what kind of subjects he's interested in and I'll line up some books that might suit."

"I will. After I get through tomorrow."

"You *will* get through tomorrow. And the outcome is not yours to determine."

"I should know that, shouldn't I? And yet here I am, keyed up like a schoolboy playing in his high-school baseball finals."

The bill came and Avery grabbed it.

"We're supposed to share on these dates, you know," she reminded him, putting her purse back.

"Not tonight."

After the server had come and gone with the point-of-sale terminal, Sarah suppressed a yawn. "I think I need to get back home. Thank you for this invitation."

Then he made the Big Blunder by letting his keenness get ahead of his restraint. "I suppose we're not too old to have a nightcap, are we?"

She cocked an eyebrow. "You mean, sex after supper? I think we are *qualified*, if that's what you mean, now that we've skillfully navigated the hand-holding stage."

Avery was taken aback by her directness, yet he held her gaze. She was making it easier for him. Ever since his libido had fired back up with

Barbara, he'd been unashamed to admit that he was a player again. She interjected before he could take the next, inevitable step. "But I don't think you're focused on lovemaking tonight. You're too preoccupied with *you*. And you've got a big day tomorrow. Let's not rush it."

"I thought you said that life was too short to wait?"

"Life is also too short to screw up the first time, because you'll have to wait an eternity for a second chance."

Avery cursed his anxiety for this misjudgment and mistiming, and which had now dampened what would have been the perfect end to a great evening. *This election has put us all off our game.*

"I admire your frankness," he admitted as he rose and held up her wrap for her.

"And I admire your gallantry," she said, wrapping the garment around her. She took his hand and they headed to the door like a sedate couple that had been together for years.

***

Brock tightened the towel around his waist and entered sauna room Number 5, marked "Private." The blast of heat was a bit much for him, and he felt his skin start to scald. He wasn't a sauna guy, but this was the ultra-private venue for his business network's meetings, a network he had successfully penetrated after much wining, dining, sponsoring, and sucking up. This sauna was a place where some of the largest nation-building and nation-destroying deals had been cooked up over the last half-century, where corporations had been bought, merged, and sold, and fortunes made for its members but never destroyed. He threw some water from the conveniently filled bowl onto the stones in the centre, and the steam hissing off the mound helped. He was sweating in no time, salty body effluent dripping off his forehead into his mouth. *Is Hell like this?*

The door slid open, ushering a refreshing blast of cool air; a bulky figure stepped in and the door closed, trapping both men inside the heat again. Bernard Phelps was naked, his towel slung over a shoulder. His bulging belly did not hide the small penis, sticking out like a rosebud. It occurred to Brock that men of power had small cocks. The need to prove oneself drove them. He tightened his own towel around his private parts, which he reserved strictly for vulnerable women in the dark.

"Good of you to see me at such short notice, and on the eve of the election."

"A de-stressing sauna is just what I need before the election," Phelps replied, hoisting himself onto a wooden seat against the wall. "You called this meeting. You said it was urgent."

"I've done my thinking. I need help with plan B."

A hiss slowly escaped Phelps, and Brock wondered at first if it was coming off the mound of stones.

"Are you sure?" Phelps was peering at him in the steam-imbued light.

"Quite sure." Brock was also pretty sure he was sweating from nervousness and was glad for the sauna's cover. In the corporate world, sweaty armpits during a shirtsleeves presentation was a sign of weakness.

"There is no going back once you take a step like this," Phelps said.

"I get that. I've come too far to turn back."

"Good. The guy I have in mind is okay, although a bit eccentric. I think he watches too many spy movies."

"I'll need him to start as soon as possible."

"No. We have to wait until after the election. Nothing can compromise my portfolio appointment."

"I'll take the timing from you. But I sense our PR has been compromised. One of my employees—"

"Ah, one of those…"

"I'll deal with the person concerned. But now I need some extended insurance."

"All right. I'll see what I can do. Throw more water on those stones, will you?"

Brock complied and the room filled with steam, blurring Phelps's image.

Through the sweltering haze, Phelps's voice droned. "Don't worry. You have finally arrived on the side of those who rule. The other side, the ruled, is made up of fodder, puppets to be manipulated and disposed of when they're no longer useful. Our role is to continuously preach the upbeat message that they swallow. When you act like that, you have emerged on the right side."

All Brock could see was the blurred image of a burly man with a small protrusion nestling on a thatch of straw-like hair between his legs. But he heard the mesmerizing message distinctly—it seared deeper than the scalding steam enveloping them.

Chapter 12

T he next morning, Avery set out at 10 a.m. on his pick-up route. It was a blustery day with rain falling and more in the forecast. Now he understood the logic of driving seniors to the polling station; it wasn't a particularly appealing day to get about on foot or on public transport.

As he drove, he noticed how much the riding had changed over the last twenty-five years. When he'd moved here in the late eighties, it had been a WASP neighbourhood; the only "ethnics" had been Greeks and Macedonians. Waves of subsequent immigration had brought West Indians, East Indians, Chinese, all using the megacity of Toronto as a springboard for making their wealth. From there they'd either span out across Canada into other communities, or stay put like Stan, build a business empire, and give back to the city that made them.

There were undesirable developments too. He passed Dempster's, a former family-style restaurant, subsequently converted into a roadhouse ten years ago. The place, once a haven for sedate family meals, had now become the haunt of cheap bands, bikers, pushers, and whores. Avery had never patronized it again after it went over to the dark side.

He pulled up at the first seniors apartment, a brownstone building from the sixties with black metal balconies that looked like battle shields. The first group was supposed to be gathered in the lobby, and he was right on time. When he buzzed and entered, there was no one around except for an elderly couple having coffee in the cavernous lobby chairs.

He ambled over to the old couple. "Would Mr. Gerry Smith and his party be around here somewhere?"

The elderly man squinted. "Gerry? He went out to vote."

The old woman with him added, "Him and a whole bunch from the darts team."

"But...there must be some mistake. I'm supposed to pick them up."

"He was in no good mood, that Gerry. Complaining about those disorganized party people who cancelled his ride."

Panic gripped Avery. "How long has he been gone?"

"Ah, dunno. Forty-five minutes maybe. He was taking the TTC. He looked mighty pissed." The man chuckled and sipped his coffee.

"Have you voted yet?"

"Nah. Not interested. They're all the same. Same broken promises all the time."

The woman put closure to Avery's invitation. "Jim and I here been voting for the Greens. They'll never win. But we figured it's our way of protesting."

There was not much more Avery could do. He walked over to a quiet part of the lobby and dialled the campaign office. A volunteer answered. "Did you guys call around and cancel the pick-ups?"

There was a hurried consultation between the volunteers, then a team leader interrupted. "Mr. Mann? Sorry to hear that, sir. We've received some calls from constituents complaining about similar phone calls they received. No one has cancelled any pick-ups at our end. I suggest you go to your next pick-up as planned. We're calling back constituents, where we're able to, to reassure them that the pick-ups are going ahead as scheduled."

Avery disconnected and rang his next pick-up contact. There was no answer. He tried the others on his list; he got voice mail twice and the final one answered in person.

"Mr. Gibbs? This is Avery Mann. I was supposed to pick you up at three p.m. today, to go to the voting booth. I was calling to reconfirm that we're still on."

There was coughing on the other side of the phone. Smoker's cough. Then the gruff voice, which had an arrhythmic rasp, said, "Don't bother. We've been and done."

"What do you mean?"

"We got a call yesterday. Told us that we had to report in person by nine o'clock this morning because the polling stations had changed, eh, and there were strict fire code regulations in the new place. So, they were taking us in batches, they said. They didn't even offer us a ride."

"And you went?" *Bloody fools.*

"Out of respect for that Barclay fellah, yeah, we went. By public transport. And you know what? The place was shut down. We figured it was some kinda joke."

"I can take you there right now, or anytime later if you prefer. To the proper place."

"Don't bother. My wife is too sick after going out in this weather. Should not have gone out in the first place. That Barclay fellah is gonna hear from me. You fellas call yourselves organized?"

Avery mumbled an apology and disconnected. This was veering from prank to sinister.

The front doors of the apartment building opened and a groups of shivering seniors ambled in through the doors.

The man named Jim having coffee with his wife called out to the person in the lead, who was striding towards the elevator, peeling off his wet jacket as he went. "Hiya, Gerry. Didja vote?"

"My ass!" Gerry replied, stabbing his finger on the call button. "That Barclay guy is going to get a piece of my mind. I'm voting no more. A bloody waste of time."

"Place was shut down," one of his companions, who was brushing her raincoat behind him, explained to Jim.

"Fellah here was looking for you," Jim said; he couldn't see Avery, who was at the other end of the lobby in the lee of a potted plant. "Came to give you a ride to the polling station." Jim was chuckling again.

"He can kiss my ass," said Gerry, stepping into the elevator. Before the doors closed, Gerry threw out one more announcement. "I'm going to spend the rest of this miserable day watching the snooker championships on TV."

***

They regrouped at campaign headquarters later that day. Crank calls had been escalating to constituents, muddying the waters, providing wrong information, confusing voters. Stan's volunteers had started calling back but the responses were often "So who do I believe, you or that other guy who just phoned?" Some calls went into voice mail, some were not picked up. The disgruntled electorate was voting in another fashion, with their silence and their absence.

Avery was able to pick up his last voters for the day, the four o'clock couple, who had been too indisposed to go out on their own in response to the robocall—as the crank calls were now being termed—that they had received earlier in the day. He made sure they were well bundled up before escorting them to his van. Out of the twenty voters allotted to him for transport during the day, Avery had only managed to ferry these two safely. Before calling it quits, he made sure to cast his own ballot, for every vote had to count now.

On the drive home, his cell-phone rang; it was Barbara.

"Did you vote?" he asked automatically.

There was an intake of breath on the other side. "Is this a good time?"

Then he realized that she was not calling about the election. Her voice sounded like it was about to break. "Sorry. I've been hauling voters around all day."

"Avery, Brock fired me today."

"What?"

"He said he didn't like the way I was handling the IPO. I think it was because he saw us together that day."

"Barbara, I'm sorry."

"I've got a generous package. But I feel kicked in the backside."

"We've all been there. But I don't understand it. I'm history. I'm not a threat to him anymore."

"But you *could* be. When we're together, we talk, and he knows that."

"Has he got something to hide? This cancer scare?"

"I didn't come across anything in the research I pulled for Damian's team. Anyway, I can't talk publicly anymore. I had to sign some papers as part of my severance. Oh, Avery…" Her voice broke and she started crying. He pulled into a strip mall because he was choking up too.

"Would Hank Smith know something?"

She stopped sobbing, but her voice was blurry. "But you said he's been long gone. Probably dead by now."

"Yeah. He must be close to ninety, if he is alive, and he probably remembers nothing anymore."

"Oh, I wish I had listened to you."

"And I guess it's too late for you to take the Abbottan Labs job now?"

"They filled it last week. I know, I know—my fault."

"Well, you made a choice. It looked like a good one at the time."

"Avery, can you come over tonight and hold my hand?"

He was tempted. After his disappointing day, a night of unbridled sex would be good to indulge in, to help him forget. It would also erase the disappointment with Sarah the night before. And yet he was reluctant. "I'll call you when I get home. I have a few more errands to run on this election thing."

"Please call me. And please come over. I need you."

He rang off and resumed his drive. The phone rang a second time. It was Paul. Rare—Paul never called; it was Avery who called Paul. He skidded into another parking spot and grabbed the phone again.

"Hi, buddy!"

"Grandpa, do you know what's good for a cut?" Paul's voice was restrained. But Avery could detect the quiver behind the formality.

"Where have you cut yourself?"

"On my hand. I was making a sandwich for dinner."

"Put some ice on it immediately to stop the bleeding. Your father or mother around?"

"Both out. Mom left the house today with her stuff." Paul's voice was now giving way to an uncontrolled sobbing. Avery did a U-turn in the middle of the main arterial road. "Hang on, kid, I'm coming over. And get that ice on the cut right away."

When he got to the Morgan residence, darkness had descended but none of the lights were on inside the house. He banged on the door. Strange, he never had been given a key to this house although Damian still had a key to Avery's house from his days as a latchkey kid. No answer. He ran around to the back. The kitchen window was open a crack. He peered through. In the half-light he made out a half-consumed loaf of bread on a cutting board. The kitchen looked barer than usual; of course—Sylvana had taken her "stuff" with her. He forced open the window and squeezed in through the opening, landing on the counter and knocking a mug onto the floor, where it splintered.

Tiptoeing around broken shards, he switched on the nearest light. There was blood on the counter—Paul's iPad was coated in it—and a trail on the floor leading out of the kitchen. He followed the bloody trail up the stairs, switching on lights as he went, until it ended outside Paul's shut bedroom door. A blood-spattered kitchen knife lay outside the door.

"Paulie?—I'm here." He opened the door and entered the dark room.

The huddled shape on the bed, smeared with dark splotches, was inert. *He's lost a lot of blood.* The left hand above the wrist was wet. Blood smeared on Avery's fingers when he held the boy's wrist. The kid had not applied the ice; probably gotten scared of the bleeding, dragged himself upstairs and passed out. *And I've left my cell phone in the van, damn!* Switching on the night lamp and tearing a pillow case, he made a tourniquet above the wrist. This was no mean slip of the knife while preparing a sandwich. Was it deliberate?

He wrapped the child in the bedsheet and carried him downstairs. He picked up the house phone to dial for an ambulance, but the line was dead. Of course, the consequences of divorce; what was working gets destroyed. He carried the boy to the van. Might be hours before an ambulance got through on election night. He drove like a maniac to the hospital.

Chapter 13

"What the hell do you mean, you needed a break after she left? Didn't your son need one too?" Avery paced the hospital waiting room yelling into his cell phone.

Damian's voice was faint over the background noise of a nightclub, and he sounded drunk. "I was owed this for a long time. The fucking months of fighting in that damned house."

"And Paul had to listen to it as well—from both of you."

"You have no idea how hard it was."

"I do. But I didn't get drunk when your mother died."

"How's Paul?" There was a hint of penitence in the distant, drunken voice.

"They've revived him, poured a pint of blood into him, and taken him up to the children's ward for the night."

"I'm coming. As soon as I can get out of here."

"Make sure you sober up before you get here." Avery disconnected before receiving a smart retort.

He took the elevator to the fourth floor, the children's ward. Paul looked pale in his room; his hand was heavily bandaged. He was wearing those stupid green hospital gowns that reminded Avery so much of Pat's last days. "Hello, buddy! You gave us a scare."

Paul gave him a sheepish grin. "Did *you* bring me here?"

"Yes. That was one big sandwich you cut."

Paul shot up in bed. "My iPad! Where is it?"

"Last time I saw it, it was covered in blood on your kitchen counter."

"Crap! Does that TV work?"

Avery stared up at the overhead TV, which looked like a boulder about to drop on their heads. The control was on the bedside table, slightly out of Paul's range of vision and reach. "Before you bury your nose in another piece of technology, we have to talk."

"I don't wanna talk."

"Well, I do."

Avery pulled up a chair and sat by the bed. Paul shrugged and sunk back in the pillows as if to say, "Grandpa isn't going to leave without his say."

"Okay," Paul muttered. "Talk."

"That wasn't an accident in the kitchen, right?"

Paul remained silent. Now he had a scowl on his face. "I was alone."

"And you were tired of being alone. So, the knife slipped, and you were sure someone would now pay attention, right? You called your father and mother and got voice mail. Then you called me. Right?"

"I texted them."

"I guess they were both busy, or didn't hear the text come in. I'm sorry. Thank God, you didn't text me."

"You never respond to texts."

"You're darned right I don't. What happened to good old-fashioned voice contact?"

"How long do I have to stay here?"

"Until the doctor says you can go home."

"Then can I come over and stay with you? I don't want to go home."

Avery bit his lip. He felt his eyes brim. "Sure. If your parents think that's okay. And I can take you to a bookshop."

"A bookshop?"

"Where the owner is building an online catalogue of books and games and needs some 'user input' from young people like you."

Paul's eyes lit up. "Gee, that sounds like fun. When can we go?"

"After you're better."

"Will you stay with me tonight?"

The door burst open and a gaunt-looking Sylvana stood in the doorway. "Baby, what happened to you?" She rushed over to the bed and fell over Paul, and Avery moved out of the way to give them space. The guilt in the room was thick as the pea soup in Paul's food tray.

She looked up from the bed, wiping a tear away. "I came as soon I was able to track you down." She looked at Avery as if looking for approval. He remained silent. "Will they let me take him home to my mother's place?"

"It's not as easy anymore, is it? You need your soon-to-be ex-husband's permission to take Paul anywhere in this new joint custody scenario."

"And where the hell is he? Drinking, I guess."

"Celebrating."

"Wait till I tell my lawyer that he put our child in danger."

Paul was beginning to cringe and shrink into the bedsheets as his mother's venting gathered steam.

Avery said, "Damian is coming over shortly. I don't think it will be helpful for Paul here, who has endured months of your fighting, to witness another fight in this hospital room."

"He can't stop me from protecting my child."

"You were *not there* to protect him. Paul contacted you via the only means of communication he engages in with you, a text, and you didn't respond. If he hadn't called me, he would have bled to death. If I were the judge, I'd say you are *both* negligent parents."

Sylvana muttered something under her breath and turned towards her son.

Avery headed for the door. "I'll leave you for a while. I'm going to the cafeteria. Want something, Paul?"

"Toblerone?" Paul looked up expectantly.

"Toblerone it is." Turning to Sylvana, Avery said, "And don't tire the boy out with your guilt. He's lost a lot of blood already."

Avery wandered through the ward and took the elevator downstairs. He felt good for having given Sylvana a piece of his mind. It had been a long time coming. People were crowded around the giant TV in the lobby.

The early polls results were coming in from Atlantic Canada. It was neck and neck between the two main parties. He had forgotten all about the election.

After buying a bar of Toblerone, he returned upstairs and was confronted by a strange scene in the corridor outside Paul's room. Sylvana and Damian were being held apart by a flustered hospital orderly. Sylvana was screaming, and Damian looked drunk and was trying unsuccessfully to creep around the orderly. Avery slipped by the entangled bodies, stepped into Paul's room, and slid the door closed. Paul had the TV on and the volume turned up. Avery tossed the chocolate bar on his bed. The boy picked it up with his good hand, sniffed it, and sighed.

"I guess your dad got here too early, eh?"

"I guess."

"Shall I open it for you?"

"No, I didn't want to eat it. I wanted to be reminded of how good it was."

They watched TV in silence for awhile. A science fiction film that had no relevance, only spectacle. The noise in the corridor abated, then ceased. After a while, the door slid open and a sober-looking Damian staggered in.

"She's gone," he announced.

"She didn't say she was leaving," Avery replied.

Paul interjected. "She was on her way out when Dad arrived. She had said goodbye to me."

Avery rose from his chair. "Here, sit down. I have to be going. I'll leave you two to bond. You can bring Paul around to my place for a few days, if you like, after they discharge him."

Damian slumped into the chair. "You mean, he has to stay the night here?"

"Yes, and you are going to spend it with him. There's a pull-out couch in that sofa. I spent three nights with you at Sick Kids when you had that infected appendix pulled, and I didn't grudge you that. Besides, it beats going back to your empty house—and *that* is something you haven't experienced yet."

"All right, all right. I'm always the bad guy." Damian had put on his hurt frown and was staring at the TV screen. Paul was avoiding eye contact with anyone in the room and was also staring up at the TV. *Joined by television. Welcome to the new splintered family.*

"Goodnight, Paul," Avery said, ruffling the boy's hair. "Call me tomorrow."

As he walked down the corridor towards the exit, Avery wondered whether he'd been harsh on his family, on Sylvana, on Damian, on little Paulie. There was something rumbling inside him, a discontent with his life, for those he had begat, for all the things he had built; they had all turned into less than desirable in his sunset years.

When he switched on his van's radio, the right-wing was pulling ahead. Majority government, they were saying. At last, the PM could do as he pleased, turn this place into the capitalist mecca he had always espoused. *Blast!* They were announcing results as they came up from ridings already counted, in no particular order. He switched off the radio, hoping that it would shut out the inevitable.

When he turned into his street, the flashing ambulance lights in front of Stanley Barclay's house made him thankful that he had taken Paul to the hospital himself and not relied on 911 on a busy night like this. Suddenly, he braked hard. Stan Barclay's house! He gunned the van, pulled into his driveway, got out, and ran across the street as two paramedics came out of the house wheeling a gurney with the patient strapped in, face covered by an oxygen mask. They ignored him and started loading the gurney quickly into the vehicle as if every second counted towards saving a life.

Lizzy Barclay stumbled out after the medics, and from her red dress and shoes Avery concluded that she had come straight from the post-election campaign party where candidates either celebrated their win or conceded defeat to round off the evening. Seeing Avery, she burst into tears. He rushed over and hugged her and her tears wet his cheek. The ambulance doors slammed, and it took off with siren blaring, leaving them hugging awkwardly in the empty driveway.

"He'll be all right," Avery said, sounding foolish.

"He come right home after his concession speech and collapsed in de bedroom."

"Let me drive you. Which hospital?"

"De General."

By the time they got to the hospital, Stan had been wheeled into intensive care. Supporters and well-wishers were trickling into the waiting area, and soon it was packed, like the campaign office must have been a few hours ago, waiting for a result that didn't go the right way.

A man in a blazer approached Lizzy and extended a business card. "I'm Alex Mendoza of the *Star*. Can you tell us what happened, Mrs. Barclay?"

Avery stepped between them and steered Lizzy towards a lounge chair. Then he addressed Mendoza. "That's what we're all here to find out. We'll have to hear what the doctor says." Avery took the journalist's card and slipped it into his pocket. The man hovered in the vicinity, like a cat watching an unfriendly dog playing with a dead mouse that was rightfully his.

Well-wishers converged on Lizzy, and she was submerged in a sea of heads. People took photos on cell-phone cameras, undoubtedly to be uploaded on social media within seconds. A young black man in sweatshirt and jeans, with long curly hair, charged into the waiting room and looked wildly around him. Avery went over and took him by the shoulder. "Sorry about your dad, Rohan. He's in intensive care. You might try and pry your mother loose from that horde."

An hour passed, with people mixing and mingling, before the crowd started to thin out. Stan's second son Dwayne, his wife, and their two daughters also arrived. Soon Lizzy was left with only immediate family, Stan's campaign secretary, and Avery. Alex Mendoza, who had managed to inveigle himself into Lizzy's orbit and extract a few minutes of her time, came around on his way out the door. "I'll be in touch. Give me a call if anything new comes up."

Dwayne, portly and with an already receding hairline, came up to Avery. "I hope he gives up this political shit after this."

"It's what defines him, Dwayne. We can't stop a person from doing what they desire."

"It will also kill him."

"Better a death than a life of unfulfilled dreams."

"Collapsing in defeat was *not* his dream."

"Look at it as falling in battle. There is honour in that, you know. We honour our soldiers for falling in action." Avery looked fondly at this young man, who once came home to play video games with Damian, not so long ago. Where had the years gone? In the flurry of activity, there had been no time to explore his own feelings about Stan's fall, but now the bile was rising in Avery's stomach and he felt he needed to go somewhere and puke.

They were mercifully interrupted when a grey-haired man in a hospital gown, with a surgical mask hanging down his face, walked in. He looked tired. Seeing and recognizing Lizzy, he walked over.

"Mrs. Barclay? I'm sorry for what's happened. I'll be brief, as I have to go back and wrap up. Your husband had a rather serious stroke. Recovery will take some time, perhaps months, even years. At this time, we're not sure how much motor or cognitive function he may have lost, as we've been focused on stabilizing him and preventing a recurrence. But as soon as we have him cleared of danger, we'll begin his rehabilitation. That's unfortunately all I can tell you at this time."

Lizzy suppressed a sob and clutched her tear-stained handkerchief. The campaign secretary started making notes—damage control spin on what had happened. Rohan intervened. "But, Doctor, are you saying that my father could have another stroke while he's in the ICU?"

"We can't rule that out, although your father is a fighter. So, we are optimistic." The doctor excused himself before further questions were thrown at him, promising to keep them updated. In parting, he said, "I suggest you all go home for the night. I'm sure it's been a long day for you. He's now in our hands."

Lizzy left the waiting room in the protective cocoon of her sons and their families, and Avery decided to leave them to their privacy. "I'm across the road. Call me if there's anything I can do. I'll check in in the morning." He knew it would be difficult to keep his bold face up for much longer. Something was giving way inside.

Alex Mendoza was in the parking lot, smoking a cigarette. "Any news?"

"They're still working on him."

"Did you see the doctor?"

Avery sucked in a deep breath. "Yes. But I prefer you wait until the official diagnosis is announced tomorrow. There's no story here. A good man ran in an election and collapsed under the stress. You're better off reporting on those robocalls."

"I'm sure we have that one covered."

Avery got into his van and slammed the door, glad for his own space at last. Mendoza waved from the other side of the glass and headed off to his car. The dashboard clock showed it was after midnight. He checked his cell phone and there were two messages. The first was from Damian to say that Paul would be discharged in the morning, and the second was from Barbara: "Thanks for standing me up, Avery. Didn't know I was such bad company." *Fuck!* He'd forgotten her completely in the rush of things. Too late to call now, she must be asleep. He felt like he had let her down, let down a lot of people tonight.

Chapter 14

He drove through empty streets. Campaign posters hung torn in places, especially the red and orange ones, and they littered the streets like the detritus of a baseball game after the winner had been decided in a fierce contest.

Dempster's, often called Dumpster's, was still open, blaring its honky-tonk music and advertising its sleaze. He belonged in a place like this tonight. On impulse, he pulled in and parked beside a pack of Harleys. The music assailed his ears as soon as he stepped through the heavy wooden door. The lighting inside was a garish yellow and green, and flashing; pool tables had replaced many of the old dining tables, and the bar had been extended to cover the length of the entire room. A three-man rock band played an unrecognizable song on a stage at the other end. Two waitresses in black cutaways that revealed skin and emphasized curves were serving crowded tables, and another in a crystal, rhinestone-studded top commanded the bar. Nothing remained of the former family restaurant, where he, Pat, and Damian had enjoyed many a Mother's Day dinner.

A burly, bearded man with a shaved head, who was standing inside the door, asked him, "Coming in?"

"Yeah."

"There's standing room only, at the bar. They'll be celebrating the election tonight."

Avery stepped up to the bar. The bikers had occupied most of the bar's counter space and were roaring at jokes that only they understood. The tables were occupied by a mix of working-class types: off-duty security guards and late-shift factory workers, judging from their uniforms and overalls; heavily rouged older women; a large group of younger people dressed in blue election campaign tee-shirts; a darts group sloshing beer, throwing darts and mostly missing; and men playing pool in earnest as if money was on the line. The rhinestone bartender doled out drinks quickly, asking for payment as she went, stuffing notes into a cash register and some into her bra. She rolled over to Avery, tucked back a blond curl and smiled through heavy red lips. "Drink, honey?"

"Double bourbon on the rocks."

The bourbon on ice, in a glass with stains on its rim, slid expertly across the counter into his hands. Right then, he couldn't care about hygiene or respectability. The anonymity this cave gave him was what he needed to hide in. The alcohol helped with the biliousness that had dogged him since running across the street into Stan's driveway. He had three double bourbons on the rocks, each time dropping a twenty-dollar bill on the counter that vanished as soon as it landed, replaced the first time with some loose change and the other two times with only a cheerful "Thanks, honey!"

The clink of gold chains and a whiff of strong perfume next to him awakened his pleasantly soused senses to the woman who had squeezed onto the stool beside him. She had dark, bushy hair and was about forty-five. "Hi!" she said, surveying him from under mascara-encrusted eyelashes. He saw ample breasts thrusting against a low-cut blouse, and her thigh pressed against his. Ms. Rhinestone slipped her a drink without enquiring and Ms. Bushy Hair winked. She picked up her drink, turned around to the burly man by the door, and raised a silent "Cheers."

"Celebrating the election?" she asked in a smoker's rasp after taking a healthy gulp. Her guttural voice made the last word sound like "erection."

"Yeah. You might say." Avery looked at her again. He felt a surge of lust. He wished he could take a whole bottle of those erection pills right now and emerge engorged, like Popeye the Sailor Man after a crateful of spinach. Lust wipes out disappointment. He would take this prostitute— for there was nothing to disguise the fact—back to his house, and fuck her. Fuck all the disappointment out of him. "Do you fuck?" he asked and was surprised at his audacity. The bourbon was talking.

She coughed over her drink, recovered, then tossed it back and started laughing. "That's the quickest sale I've ever made."

"Your place or mine?" He was enjoying the repartee. Never in his life had he done this, and with such brevity and brusqueness.

"I don't make house calls. My pad is above this joint. Whenever you're ready."

"Lead on, Ms. Horatio," Avery said, downing his drink and sliding— nearly falling—off his stool.

She left her drink unfinished, took his hand, nodded at the burly man, and led Avery through a door beside the washrooms up a narrow staircase to the second floor. Several doors led off a narrow corridor.

Avery hiccupped. "I didn't know this honeymoon paradise was available so near to home. Why travel to the Caribbean?"

"You're welcome, any time." She opened the second door, pushed him in, and flicked on the room's light. It was a box, with space only for a fake-fur-covered bed and a vanity table and stool. It smelled of sweat, air freshener, and something sulphurous. "Time to freshen up," she said, grabbing the aerosol container and shooting a few lemon-scented sprays into the air.

He stood, wedged between the bed and the vanity, feeling stupid and awkward.

She sat on the stool and threw off her skimpy top to reveal breasts squeezed into fullness by a push-up bra. She left on the chains and the heavy bangles. "It's fifty for a blow job, a hundred for a fuck, and two-fifty for the full course, including the arse. Cash up front."

"Do you take a credit card?" He was trying to hide his nervousness now that he was obligated to buy.

"You wouldn't want to trust me with your credit card, honey." She started to peel off her bra, then stopped. "You're not changing your mind, are you?" The arching of her plucked and painted eyebrows, and the parting of her thin red lips, gave her a Cruella De Vil look.

He was out of his league here. This was not his game, and he realized it too late. He fished out his wallet. He had three twenties left. "I spent my cash down at the bar. Let's settle this. I'll pay you fifty plus a generous tip for the blow job that never was." He threw the three twenties on the bed and lurched towards the door.

"Oh, that's a shame. You have difficulty getting it up? I got stuff for that too. Might cost you a bit extra." She quickly grabbed the notes and slid them into her bra, readjusting the straps.

Her words stung him. *So, this is what it is to grow old.* But he had come here voluntarily, seeking the ignominy that was now being heaped upon him.

He threw open the door. "I'll show myself out."

"Watch the stairs. And take a taxi home. If you come again, I'll blow you for free to get you started."

He slammed the door behind him. All he heard was the clinking of her bangles behind the thin wall, and the grunts and sighs coming from other rooms. As he staggered down the corridor for the stairs, these new sounds became amplified in his consciousness, now robbed of its blinding lust and replaced with a deep disgust.

∗∗∗

He drove like the flames of hell were about to engulf him, wanting to get away, to escape from the messes he seemed to be getting into. He did not stop at home, but headed straight for the cottage. With the roads wide open at this time of the morning, 3 a.m., he figured he'd get to the cottage before sun-up. And he would stay there until this sense of being a loser had dissipated.

The events that had transpired over the past forty-eight hours washed over him like waves in a benign ocean that steadily increased in ferocity and drowned the most unsuspecting swimmer: the botched date with Sarah, standing up Barbara in her time of need, falling for the robocalls,

Damian's marriage finally ending, Paul's attention-seeking act, the election loss, Stan's collapse, and finally the whore who had humiliated him. He was driving through a long, metaphoric night, it seemed, and it wasn't over yet, if indeed it ever would be. He wanted to hold someone responsible for his misfortunes. And the faces that swam in his vision were Martin Brock, Norman Samuels, and Bernard Phelps and...and...all those people who promoted material gain over everything else. The prostitutes and call-centre robots and unemployed executives and marriage breakdowns and health breakdowns and suicides, all attributable back to these people who embodied greed. But he was one of them too. How dare he berate his son for selfishness when he himself was not averse to buying sex for personal gratification? As he drove on auto-pilot along familiar roads to his cave by the lake where he could lick his wounds, he hated himself.

He stopped in Peterborough for coffee at an all-night truck stop. What he really needed was another drink. But there was an OPP cruiser in the parking lot, and he had passed another on the highway, so he figured they were out early, hunting for speeding drunks like him to meet their budget quotas. And they wouldn't need a breathalyzer to confirm that he was over the limit.

He drove slower when he resumed his journey. The coffee helped somewhat to abate the effects of the booze. But he was feeling like shit.

He sighed in relief when he passed the grain silo and the windmill. He left the car outside the cottage gate and hauled himself uphill. He sighed again when he dropped his pants and sent a stream of piss into the roots of the oak tree in his yard, then farted loudly to signal his satisfaction. It was dark, but early birds were starting their ruckus already. In the dying moonlight reflecting off the lake, he found the keyhole after several attempts. He had no supplies on him, or clothes, but he remembered that he had left some belongings and dry goods behind from his last visit. He flicked the light switch but remained in darkness. Power failure? Since he was using his own electricity from the solar panels, something must have gone wrong with the connections—squirrels, most likely. That's why he had an oil-powered generator too. But he was damned if he was going to fiddle with either of them at this godforsaken hour.

He groped in the darkness until he found the candles and the matchbox that he kept in the niche above the stove. He lit several candles and stuck them in various corners of the living room. The cottage was stuffy, and he opened a window, letting in a chilly breeze from the lake. He left his coat on. He would sleep in it until daylight awoke him. He threw himself on the couch, but his mind was doing somersaults, repeating the events of the day, aided by the coffee he had recently drunk. He needed alcohol to counter the caffeine. He rose, stumbled into the kitchen, and found a half-empty bottle of scotch. He drank from the bottle, and the burn of the liquid down his already parched throat felt good, it felt like the punishment he deserved. He fell down on the couch again.

Day broke rapidly here, and light was starting to brighten the room when the empty bottle fell out of his hands and clinked on the floor.

But he was blissfully unaware of his surroundings. He had floated into a better place, a place where he was a young man with dreams and innocent ambitions, with a young son and a devoted wife, and an ordered life. He was playing in the garden with his toddler son, then bicycling with Pat beside some beach they had gone to, then...the images kept appearing and dissolving only to be replaced by others; they were fragmented and happy ones.

The light was suddenly too bright and there was that stifling smell that turned his dreams into nightmares. He was in a fog and he was suffocating. He shot up from the couch, instinctively, fearing the worst. It took him a moment to get his bearings. The living room was filled with smoke. At a glance, he took in the curtain on fire by the open window, obviously blown into the path of a burning candle by the wind, and the trail of fire that had spread around the room. He was gasping for breath by the time he pulled himself through the front door and collapsed in the yard. And his cell phone, where the heck would that be at this time? Inside the cottage or inside his van? He couldn't remember. He couldn't go back inside, so he had to head for the van and get help. Would the neighbours see and come over? But the cottages here were far apart, and the neighbours might not be at their cottages, for it was mid-week. When he got to the van and looked back at the house, smoke was emerging in a dark trail through the windows. No cell phone in the van. He was going to have to drive for help. And he was pretty darned drunk.

Mercifully, he had left the keys in the ignition. He reversed violently, skidded, and took off down the narrow, pot-holed path that led to the main road. He took the first turn dangerously and swerved to avoid a boulder that marked the next one—too late. The van hit the rock and tried to mount it. He heard a cracking noise as the wheel bearing broke, and the van's bottom scraped stone and wedged itself on top of the monolith, engine revving. He threw the vehicle into reverse and it peeled back off the rock with more scraping and cracking. But when he had all four wheels on the ground again and tried to head out, the front left wheel wobbled and the van tilted dangerously on that side. He switched off the ignition and staggered out of the van. This vehicle was going nowhere but to a repair shop. He left it and teetered towards the main road, ten minutes by car, an eternity by foot. And with every step he took, he was not only walking away from his dream cottage, it was burning itself to the ground. *This fucking night is not over yet.*

He met a fire truck coming towards him fifteen minutes later and hailed it down. The neighbour across the lake had seen the blaze and phoned 911, the firemen told him. And why hadn't he walked in the opposite direction towards the wetlands, over to the other neighbour who lived only a kilometre away instead of trying to make the journey into town himself? He couldn't answer that question. They helped him into the truck, but the lead fireman immediately smelled him and said, "There'll be some explaining to do later, but let's get this sucker of a fire under control first."

The second fireman, a little more sensitive than the first, leaned over and asked if he was all right, and could they get him something.

"I'm doing pretty fine for a guy who's lost everything in a couple of days. You'll find my van without a wheel, a bit up the road. Perhaps you could call for a tow truck."

He passed out from exhaustion before they got to the blazing cottage.

Chapter 15

They met on the boardwalk at the Beaches. The day was ending and the light suspect, distorting shapes and features. A few strollers walked dogs, carrying plastic bags in their hands; the ice cream vendor was shutting down his cart for the day, and the hardy souls who had braved the water on this unusually warm day in early June were coming in and grabbing towels.

They converged from different ends of the boardwalk: he from the flat eastern end; the tall man with a ponytail, wearing shades and a soft leather jacket, had the CN Tower and downtown office skyscrapers as a backdrop. In the fading light, the shades were unnecessary, but they completely hid the eyes, and Brock was certain he wouldn't pick out the man again in an identification line without the dark glasses and the ponytail.

But the accent was distinct—German—despite many years in Canada, per the bio that had been fed to him.

"I'll make it quick," Brock said, after they had exchanged a codeword to make the connection.

"*Ja*. Time is money." The German's eyes were boring into him from behind those shades, Brock was sure, for the head didn't move.

"The money was transferred yesterday."

"*Ja*. That is why I am here. You are serious."

Brock extended the envelope to the man. "You will find the information you are looking for inside."

The man broke the seal.

"Not here," Brock said, glancing around. Only a dog walker was in the vicinity, but she was walking a Dobermann away from them.

"I like to see if I have all the information. Once, I eliminated the wrong person."

"I thought you didn't make mistakes."

"They forgot to tell me she had an identical twin, who was living with her at the time."

The man pulled out two postcard-sized photographs from the envelope and studied them. "They are old. Why do you want them...out of the way?"

"We don't have to discuss that. I pay for your services and that includes not asking unnecessary questions."

"I need to know if they are worth scrubbing. Have they done bad things in their lives? Makes it easier."

"They have secrets."

"*Ach.*"

"The rest of the money will be transferred to your offshore account when I have confirmation that both...both...are out of the way."

The mouth parted below the shades and a string of pearly white teeth glistened in the gathering gloom. A man who looked after his personal hygiene. "*Ach.* It will be so. *Auf Wiedersehen!*"

Brock suppressed a shiver after the man melted into the dusk. This was a stage he had never wanted to get to, but it lay along the inevitable trajectory upon which he had placed his professional life. They say that children who torture animals eventually kill them, and then graduate to bigger kill, such as humans. He didn't have any children, despite three wives, all of whom had been interested only in the good life. But now he felt like the kid who had grown up killing animals.

He returned to his car and cranked up the heat, despite the warm spring night. He was shaking, with release and relief. Bernard Phelps had snagged the health portfolio, but Brock couldn't rely on the party brass. It would be far easier for them to throw Phelps under the political bus and disavow any complicity if any pharma-related scandal kicked up, now that the robocalls incident was making headlines. The German, Wolfgang

Sauer—one of many aliases used by the man, or maybe that *was* his real name—was a contract killer who operated across international borders. He came with a stellar track record, a name, and a form of contact that was only traded in places such as the ultra-secret confines of a sauna in a private downtown club for high-profile executives. Never via email, never on the internet, never on Facebook.

***

The old man looked up from his labours on Vancouver Island. One pull of the handle of the newly installed cable and lever system attached atop the hives would raise the covers of all his boxes simultaneously, rattle the frames, and the bees would leave his care forever. He had puzzled over how he would provide the bees with their ultimate freedom. One hive box at a time? No, that was tedious. This finale had to be like a Canada Day fireworks display, a grand exodus that he could wave farewell to and which would be complete. And what better time to do it than on Canada Day next month.

The house had sold within a week of being listed, for $25,000 above the asking price, and the new owner, who was also, conveniently, a recreational beekeeper, had bought his hives and the contents of his work shack, so they didn't have to be removed. But the old man had not included his bees in his sale to the buyer. *Let him get his own bees.* He would leave the new owner the frames of honey, which he would remove from the hives' supers and store in his work shack the day before he left for Germany; the new owner, who would take possession the following day, would be responsible for extracting the honey from the frames and for packaging and selling—painstaking work that Hank had done for the last ten years. That was the arrangement.

The retirement home in Guelph—his first hometown after arriving in Canada—had a space for him in early August. It was all arranged: he would fly to Germany on July 1 after his own "fireworks display" and travel about the Fatherland for a month, visit old haunts, bury old ghosts that haunted him in that now-restored country, and return to Guelph to live out his days in peace.

The expected onslaught of media vultures after his letter was mailed a month ago hadn't materialized—yet. Well, if it didn't happen, tough! He had let the secrets of the past go. Writing the letter had been cathartic and was his act of contrition. That was what mattered. Now he had to get the house ready for the new owner, who would take possession on July 1 and release him from this land. Yet, he secretly hoped there *would* be a reaction to his letter.

And there were a few things that he had to attend to before he could leave. Old books had to be donated to the second-hand bookstore; crockery, and knickknacks had to go to the Re-Store; letters and photographs had to be burned. And that pesky branch from the oak tree that had fallen last week had to be gotten rid of—maybe he'd chop it into firewood as a gift to the new homeowner. Normally Bob, who maintained the property for him, would do this, but this was a job he wanted to do himself; a gift must come from one's own hand. And there were of course, the papers. They would have to be moved if no one came for them.

But all that was for later. He was tired now and he was going indoors to rest. Somehow, he felt that everything would fall into place.

Chapter 16

"It doesn't matter whether I was drunk or not. The wind blew the curtain into the flame while I was asleep. That's what started the fire."

Avery was sitting in his living room in Scarborough, across from the suited young man with his laptop open and papers spread out on the table.

"But you were also charged with driving a vehicle under the influence," the man countered. He was swarthy, South Asian, used to wheeling and dealing with insurance claimants who set ailing small businesses and property on fire to benefit from the disasters, Avery gauged. *He's been to the school of hard knocks for claims adjusters.*

"You should consider yourself lucky that I do all my insurance—property, vehicle and life—with your firm. You've been making money off me for over thirty years. This is the first claim I've made, and you're giving me all this grief?"

"It's a pretty sizable claim overall, Mr. Mann. Your vehicle repair cost only about five thousand, but the cottage is going to cost over a hundred thousand to replace. That would be more than all the premiums you've paid in thirty years on both your properties—the cottage and this house— combined."

"And if you add up only what I've paid on my auto insurance over the years, without a single claim, that will more than cover the replacement of my cottage. So, what's the beef?"

"We do not mix classes of insurance, Mr. Mann."

"Then why are you mixing my drunk driving with a fire in my cottage?"

They traded arguments back and forth for another fifteen minutes, until Avery got exasperated and threw up his hands. "Okay, enough of this. I've signed all the papers you need. I'll look forward to your reply in a couple of weeks so that I can rebuild my cottage. I got my vehicle out of the garage only yesterday, thanks to all your waffling."

The young man shut his laptop and began putting his papers away into a briefcase. "We'll see what we can do, Mr. Mann."

After the adjuster had departed, Avery inspected, for the zillionth time, the photographs taken of his cottage, or the ruin that his cottage now was: only the walls were left standing. The couch, a family heirloom, on which he had spent many hours of indolence, was a pile of ashes. Family photographs, many of his parents' early days in Germany, burned out of recognition. A dream, gone up in smoke. So much for retirement planning; it only assuaged the soul, not the pocketbook. Tears welled in his eyes. He had tried not to look at these pictures when they were first presented to him a month ago, but today had been the day of "deep diving" into his insurance claim, as the adjuster had termed it, and there had been no respite during the exercise. Now he was also being treated as a suspect claimant.

He glanced through the window at the house across the street. Stan was seated in a wheelchair on his front lawn, his head at an awkward angle, with a bib around his neck. Stan had come home from hospital a week ago. He was paralyzed on his right side and his speech was slurred. Lizzy took him daily for rehabilitation exercises, after which Stan sat out on his lawn and stared into space. He had to be fed, purees and juices only, as his jaw muscles didn't fully work, and he drooled.

Avery's gloom lifted, only slightly. *At least I am not as badly off as Stan.* He waved to Stan and saw the man slowly lift his good hand in acknowledgement. Cars passed by on the street but none slowed or stopped for Stan. Where were the Doug Sanderses, the Asif Mikanis, and the John Doddses who had been in and out of the Barclay residence prior to the election? Gone to find a new leader to pledge their allegiance to? And yet, there had been a time, not too long ago, when Stan couldn't step out of his house without being mobbed by supporters and hangers-on.

Avery decided he would go out later and visit. He would read to Stan from the newspaper, articles highlighting questions about the robocalls scandal that were now being raised in parliament. But first he had to attend to some pending business.

The phone rang. It was Sarah. She had called regularly since he had given her the news about the incident at the cottage. She had unexpectedly become the only person in whom he could confide. He hadn't told Damian of his disaster until his son called to ask why he hadn't come over to pick up "the kid." And Damian's response, after Avery had told him why, had been "Did you take a full inventory for the claim?" A gentler, "Sorry to hear what happened, Dad," would have been better, but it wasn't forthcoming. Sarah, on the other hand, had been a good listener as he had unburdened his shock, anger, fear, and sadness, in no particular order. She hadn't judged or offered solutions; she had merely listened sympathetically. He wondered what he would unburden today, but she caught him short with a question soon after they had exchanged greetings.

"Now that your van is operational again, when are you bringing Paul around to the shop? I've purchased the iPads, attached to cables so they don't get stolen, and I'm planning a mini launch party for the kids to try out the equipment."

"Ah, yes..." he was groping for the answer. Paul was another broken promise. Avery's assurance that' he'd keep the boy for a few days after he came out of hospital had never transpired because of the cottage fire and its aftermath of home inspections, claims reports, vehicle repairs, and a brief court appearance for drunken driving (where the judge had been kind to Avery, for he had been technically drinking *inside* his home and had been forced outdoors and into his vehicle only due to the fire). Avery had withdrawn contact with everyone, except by phone, given that, until only yesterday he had been without a vehicle, and had turned down the offer of a rental during the gap. He knew why he was staying away: he felt the guilt of letting people down, the shame of seeking temporary release with a whore, and for being a drunken, irresponsible senior citizen who had blown up his own retirement—there was no blaming Damian or Brock or Phelps or anyone else this time.

"Yes, I'll ask Paul," he replied sheepishly.

"And when do I get to see *you*? These phone conversations are getting a bit, well... boring."

He sighed. He didn't want to see anyone—didn't she get it? Now with the cottage gone, his suburban home had become his cave.

"I'm sorry that I was unable to take you out to visit my cottage. I guess I left it a bit late."

"You'll build another one."

He didn't share her enthusiasm. It would take a long time before the cottage was replaced, judging from the look on that claims adjuster's face. Besides, he had lost his appetite for cottage life. At best, if his claim was approved, he could get a replacement cottage, but it would not have his touch, and would be devoid of the love and sweat he'd poured into the original; at worst, they'd deny his claim and he'd sell the land and retire to this house in Scarborough with his nest egg further shrunk. Neither sounded like interesting options. There had to be something else now, a new departure, but he didn't want to tell her that, because he didn't know what that replacement should be.

"I'll bring Paul out as soon as I can get things arranged with his parents. It's a bit complicated now with their separate custody arrangements."

"Please make it soon. As they say, at this stage of life, we don't have all the time in the world anymore."

He promised again and hung up. He looked back at the phone. Funny, today she had been upbeat, impatient, whereas ever since the fire she had been sympathetic and understanding. Was she signalling to him that there was a time to grieve and a time to move on, and that now it was time to move on? It was nice to be needed, despite her medicine being strong.

He brewed a cup of coffee and took it to his nook with the daily newspaper, which he hadn't read yet. Lizzy was wheeling Stan indoors for his afternoon nap. The flowers in the Barclay front yard—gardening was Lizzy's lifelong hobby when she was not volunteering somewhere—were beginning to wilt in the noon-day sun.

After reading the latest on the robocalls, he turned to the business news out of habit and glanced through the career appointments. A tinge of regret coursed through him whenever he came across pictures of grey and balding men still ascending corporate ladders. A photograph of a youngish Mark Preston stared back at him: appointed new Canadian CEO of Medico-Bio, a European genetic medicine company opening up a presence in Canada. Mark's past HR expertise was being touted as a key attribute being brought to the fledgling Canadian operation, which was seeking new talent as its first order of business.

Avery phoned Mark at his new contact address and got his voice mail immediately. Mark must be a one-man show trying to set up things with no budget for assistants and other corporate trimmings. Avery knew what he wanted to say in his voice message and didn't let Mark's absence deter him. "Congratulations, Mark. This is Avery Mann. I read about your new appointment. Well deserved! Now you get to run your own show. I may have someone for you, as you are, no doubt, scouting for talent at present." He left his phone number and disconnected.

Then he opened his email. The usual junk mail from Viagra merchants and dating sites. His online forays into erectile prolongation and single women must have got him pegged. How quickly one's online search results get aggregated into an online profile, rendering one an advertising demographic. He felt ashamed of where marketing as a discipline had gravitated. There was also an email from an unusual source, someone he was not expecting to hear from: Olga Beckmeyer.

Dear Avery,

I know this note will come as a surprise, but we live in surprising times. I retired from Sand, as I told you, as part of my final restructuring assignment. A month afterwards, I fell ill. It was as if the cancer was waiting in the wings, but unable to attack me while I was busy doing the devil's work. However, that is not what I am writing to you about, for I am taking my treatments for the illness, and that will take whatever course it takes. The chemo makes me very tired and confused at times, though, but now as I don't have to go anywhere, I spend most of my days at home, sleeping. And it is very strange that in my chemo-dreams I live through all my days at Sand, for it is the only life I have known for the last thirty years.

I received a letter a few weeks ago – and this is what I want to discuss with you – from a very surprising source. I couldn't deal with it immediately as I was trying to cope with my treatments. I cannot deal with it by email either as the information is too sensitive and is also in hard copy. Can we meet? My home address is below. I think you will find this information of help to you and it will shed light on a lot of things we took for granted. I am home most of the day, and available if I am not asleep.

Olga

Avery stared for a long time at the note. An eerie tingle crept down his back. He immediately wrote back.

Dear Olga,

I'm sorry to hear about your predicament. I hope you will develop some hobbies when you are through with your treatments. I should know, because I never developed any myself. Instead, I built a cottage in my spare time, and it went up in flames last month. But that's another story. I am intrigued by the surprising letter you received. I can call over the day after tomorrow, Sunday at 11 a.m. I hope that will work. Let me know.

Regards!

Avery

No sooner had he pressed "send" than the phone rang. Mark was returning his call. After exchanging greetings and congratulations, Avery got down to business. "Mark, do you remember Barbara Spencer?"

"Sure—your protégée."

"Not any more. Brock fired her last month."

"What? Last I heard—before my exit—he had her working on their IPO project."

"He changed his mind. She's now looking for work, and I said I'd see what I could do."

"Why hasn't she called me directly?"

"Well, your announcement just came out. And she's grieving her demise at Sand. *I* am still grieving after five years, although I hate to admit it."

"I understand. It happened to all of us."

"But you bounced back pretty fast."

"I'd been working on the Medico-Bio deal for some time, while I was at Sand. When I saw Brock's next round of cuts coming up, I inveigled my name into the ring, so I could get some paid vacation time until my next challenge. I guess it worked out differently for me."

"Smart man! I'll ask Barbara to get in touch, if she's interested."

"Please do. She'll be an easy slide into the role of PR director."

After he hung up, Avery composed an email to Barbara:

Dear Barbara,

This note will come out of the blue, but I wanted to apologize for standing you up on the night of the election. A lot of things happened on that "night of my long knives," as I call it. Suffice to say that I lost my cottage, my van, nearly lost my grandson, and we lost the election, and my candidate lost his health and is now reduced to a near-vegetative state. But we all come back. We have to. I hope you are coming back from your job loss too.

I have thought about the two of us, and I think the best role for us is that of mentor and mentee. When we crossed the line to be something more, something else, it led to feelings of inadequacy, jealousy, hurt, avoidance, and other negatives that I never before experienced with you, for ours has always been a positive relationship. I'm sorry for crossing the line, although I do not regret the things we did together when there was no line separating us.

This note is to ask for your forgiveness for any hurt I may have caused. I would also like to offer a glimmer of hope, for that is what we were trained as leaders to provide: hope. Mark Preston has emerged as CEO of Medico-Bio, a genetics medicine company, and he is looking to build a new Canadian team. I mentioned you to him, and he is interested. I don't know what you have done in the last month since we talked, but if job search is still on your priority list, please give him a call. He is waiting to hear from you. His contact details are below.

I wish you all the best. Do keep in touch and let me know how your next career move progresses. As your mentor, I am always available and interested.

Regards!

Avery

He felt relieved after pressing "send." He felt more relieved when he saw Olga's reply in his inbox saying that Sunday at 11 a.m. would be okay to meet.

Time for lunch, he thought. A productive morning. The best one this entire month since the fire.

The doorbell rang. This annoyed him. Not another Jehovah's Witness, or someone selling consumer gas when his stomach was growling! When Avery opened the front door, a small figure stood on the doorstep. The half-sleeved Toronto Blue Jays jersey revealed pink skin on the forearm where the bandages had recently come off.

"Paul! What are you doing here?"

"PD Day."

"But how did you get here?"

"I took the TTC. Dad doesn't know."

Avery's eyes widened as he opened the door wider to let his grandson in. "I bet he doesn't. Your parents ferry you everywhere. Or I do."

"Well, they don't have the time anymore. You don't either."

"I didn't have a vehicle until yesterday."

"You could have taken the TTC."

Avery was struck by the boy's directness and stumbled over his next words. "I guess. . .I guess, I could have. Have you had lunch yet? Not sure what's in the fridge, but I'm sure I could rustle up something."

"Pizza?"

"I'll check the freezer."

Avery found a solitary pizza in the freezer, one of his relief supplies. He turned on the oven, stripped the pizza of its wrapping, and embellished it with what was left in the fridge: some dried-out mushrooms, a spring onion, salami, and cocktail olives. He sprinkled lots of oregano and garlic powder on the thawing pizza and stuck it in the oven. He poured two glasses of orange juice and took them into the living room. Paul was studying the pictures lying on the dining room table.

"Pizza will be a few minutes." Avery handed Paul a glass and placed his hand on the boy's shoulder. "I'm sorry for not coming around earlier. I guess I was preoccupied."

The boy took the glass absentmindedly and continued studying the pictures. "Dad told me about your cottage. It's all gone, isn't it?"

"Insurance will build me a new one."

"It's not the same, Grandpa." Paul looked up and there were tears in his eyes. "When I saw blood all over my iPad, I knew it wouldn't be the same iPad again. I hardly use it anymore."

Avery put his hand on Paul's shoulder. His own eyes were moist.

"Is that why you came to see me today?"

"When you wouldn't come to our home to visit, I figured you were hurting pretty bad too."

"Yeah. But I'll get over it. We get over most things. Like you *will* get over your dad and mom."

"I miss Mom. I mean, I don't miss *living* with her, but I miss her being around. Do you miss Grandma?"

"Yeah. But she is around in this house. Don't you sense her presence?"

"Yes, I do. But it's not the same as before. And you've gotten rid of all the family pictures on the walls in this room. No, it's not the same."

"I thought it was time for a change. You know, even if they build me a new cottage, I don't think I'll be moving out there either."

Paul's face brightened up and he sniffed back his tears. A smile broke through. "That's great! I mean...like, I'll get to see more of you then, right?"

"Yeah. And I'm pretty proud that you got on that bus today. You did better than me."

Later, they were finishing their pizza when his cell phone rang. Avery walked with the phone into his bedroom and shut the door. It was Damian, and he sounded agitated.

"Can you take Paul for a bit? As you've been promising since Syl left? I have to go out of town early tomorrow for a couple of days."

"Do you have his mother's permission?"

"She's not supposed to know. If she knows that I've dumped him on you while he's supposed to be with me, I'll be hearing from her lawyer again."

"What's so important that you have to go out of town?"

"We're having an offsite meeting to wrap up the Sand IPO. The due diligence is over, now the sales show is about to go on the road."

"Tomorrow is the weekend. Have you become a slave labourer now?"

"It's a twenty-four-seven, three-hundred-and sixty-five-days-a -year world in my business. Especially when we're so close to going public."

Damian's tone sounded genuine, and Avery quickly dismissed the mental image of a naughty weekend for the newly "liberated" corporate executive. "You're going to have this parental conflict with the next deal, and the next..."

"Please, Dad—can I not count on your help, and your confidence?" Damian's plea was sincere, bordering on frantic.

Avery lowered his voice. "What if Paul himself accidentally lets on to his mother that he spent time with me?"

"He won't. He's had two spells with Syl this month and he doesn't like living with her, and if his reward for him ratting on me is that he gets to spend *all* his time with her, I know how the kid's going to vote. Besides, he gets to see you only when he's with me and he's not going to blow that."

"All right. As a matter of fact, he's here with me now. I picked him up from your place a little earlier." Avery hoped the lie would stick. It did. Damian's next words were, "Does he have any clothes?"

"No. But we could come around later and pick some up."

"Thanks, Dad."

Avery was starting to be of use again. He disconnected the phone and let the feeling wash over him. Suddenly he was coming to the aid of several people who needed him.

Yes, and he'd definitely go over to Stan's later in the afternoon after everyone had risen from their nap and Paul had settled in front of the TV. Stan was another guy who needed him. Stan, even if it was only so he could nod and listen to stories. For most of his life Stan had done the talking, at political rallies, at party meetings, in his restaurants, and in his home. Now it was Stan's time to listen. Avery wondered what wisdom his friend was silently gathering that could not be shared back with others like himself who were busy "doing," because the doers had no time to listen.

Chapter 17

When Avery and Paul drove to Forest Hill to pick up Paul's things that evening, there was a "For Sale" sign up on the lawn. Damian was sitting on the front porch in a jogging suit and sweatband. A can of beer sweated by his side. Despite his athletic apparel, the paunch threatening on all sides revealed a life of corporately paid fine dining. The evening sun cast a warm glow on the neighbourhood of wrought-iron fences and forbidding gates. The tragedies of the rich were well hidden, well…except for Damian's. Avery got out of the van and walked up the driveway. Paul rushed past him, threw a "Hi Dad" to his father, and ran through the front door, slamming it behind him.

"Good to see you keeping fit, despite your hectic life," Avery said, taking a seat on the steps beside his son. "Not sure about the beer, though."

"Help yourself. There's more in the fridge."

"No thanks! I drank enough for a whole year on election night."

Damian shrugged, smiling, but his lips drooped. "Actually, I was being kind of nostalgic. I'll be leaving here soon, after the house sells. All my attempts at home and family are coming to a close." This reflective tone from Damian was unusual. *It's the beer, and he is finally growing up!*

"Well, you'll build again. I feel the same with the cottage. One errant candle was all it took to blow up my dream."

"I need a win."

"The IPO?"

"It's the ticket. I'll be forty in a few months. If I don't make partner within the next year, I'm going to be on the hit list."

"That hit list mark used to hover around fifty years when I was in the corporation. The age of promotion gets younger and younger, it seems.

'Bring 'em in young, suck out the best years of their lives, and spit 'em out like sucked-out olive pits.' Business is a game of tennis—all balls and rackets.'"

"I wish they hadn't both come at the same time—the divorce and the promotional jitters. I guess I didn't realize how much the divorce took out of me. Fighting at close quarters, inside this house for eight months, was murder. I enjoyed the fight while it lasted, though. But when it ended, I only felt the fatigue."

"I guess divorce is like a death."

"Except that the corpse lives on to haunt you. Or take you to court for neglectful parental behaviour."

"Talking about parental behaviour, would it be okay if I took Paul to a bookstore tomorrow?"

"Works for me. Not sure he's interested in books, though."

"This woman...lady...who runs the bookstore, has a knack for storytelling. I think she would be able to work some magic on Paul."

Damian craned his neck at Avery. "Must be some special kind of lady. You seeing someone?"

Avery blushed.

"Come on, Dad. You should. It's been a while."

"She's a friend. I don't bounce back as fast as you do. In a way, I envy her. She's trying to define her life on her own terms by running her own business with its myriad challenges. For myself, I was a corporate slave, a glorified clerk, and now it's too late to redefine myself."

Damian drained his beer. "Join the club."

"You're young. You can regroup and relaunch yourself."

"Young? That's another thing that's pissing me off: having to look impressive for women again. They say that the shaved look is in, everywhere. Chest, pits, balls—everywhere. Painful. There's an app for consensual sex, they tell me. There's an app for everything: dating, dining, drinking. It takes a lot of work to figure out and I'm fifteen years out of practice."

"Well, if it's any consolation, I'm about forty-five years out of practice. And I'm not shaving for anyone."

They were interrupted by Paul, who came out on the porch. He was dragging a stuffed duffel bag behind him. "Can we go now?"

Avery rose and dusted off his pants. He reached out and gave his grandson a hug. "Yes, we can head back home. Have to stop for some groceries on the way. Haven't been keeping tabs on my fridge these days."

"Bye, Dad!" Paul threw the parting at his father without much enthusiasm.

"Bye, fella. Don't give your Gramps a hard time. And if Mom calls—"

"I know. 'Grandpa took me to the movies and I decided to stay over.'"

As Paul was loading his bag into the van, Avery gripped Damian on the shoulder. "You have a good meeting tomorrow. Do the best you can. That's all you *can* do. Fate and circumstance determine the result, not you—remember that." For some strange reason he felt he had been given that same advice recently by Sarah, only he hadn't taken it.

As they drove away, Avery glanced back at his son in the rear-view mirror, sitting forlorn on the porch, as if staring at the looming mid-life crisis that was inevitably heading his way.

***

"I've brought the lad," Avery announced when he pushed through the door of Brook's Books, Paul in tow. It was just past 10 a.m. and they had been waiting in the van, parked across the street, for the "Open" sign to switch on inside the store window.

Sarah, in a sleeveless summer dress, left the cash counter and came over immediately. "Well! It's nice to see *you*." She was looking directly at Avery and the longing in her eyes made his heart swoon.

"This is Paul."

Paul extended his hand to Sarah tentatively. Sarah gave him a hug instead. "Hello, Paul. Welcome to our mess. But we have some books and stuff that you might find interesting." She took him by the shoulder and gently walked with him over to a circular gated area that had been recently constructed: a reading pod beside the stage. Avery looked around, and saw there had been modifications made since he was last here. An artificial fireplace had been installed at one end of the room with the book shelves moved back, leaving more space in the centre, and the darker colours had given way to pastels. The decorators hadn't quite finished, because paint buckets, rollers, and a ladder lined the far wall. The room looked larger and brighter.

Paul got busy immediately on the new iPads tethered around the reading pod.

"Grandpa, this is cool—the latest iPad2 models!"

Sarah smiled at Avery. "As you can see, I've sunk more money into this last gasp of making my bookshop viable. I hope young readers are as enthusiastic as Paul. The selections that come up on the iPads are all available as paperbacks in the store. Hopefully, there's cross-pollination, as you call it."

Turning to Paul, she said, "The reading pod is not officially open yet, so don't draw too much attention to it."

"Or *do* draw attention," Avery said. "Imagine the hype he could create if your other customers see him inside right now. They'll be fighting to get in."

She laughed this time. "I guess I don't think like a marketer. My reopening is next week and I won't be happy until everything is ready." She motioned with her head towards the painters' implements. "Let me get you a coffee while Paul plays with the new tools."

She traded places with the clerk behind the coffee counter, who went into the bookshop to replace Sarah. Coffee patrons were already coming in for their morning fix and most of the tables were occupied. "I wish it were the same in the bookshop," Sarah whispered as she went behind the counter to make him a latte. He sat on a counter stool, watched her movements, and knew that he had missed her.

"I have Paul for the weekend," Avery said, when Sarah brought him his coffee. "His father's out of town."

"Let's see—and the boy's mother doesn't know?" Sarah crooked an eyebrow.

Avery shrugged. "Something like that. I'm still getting used to this cloak and dagger stuff."

"But you are a willing accomplice."

"I didn't know what to do with him, so I thought bringing him here would be a good idea."

When Sarah switched places with the clerk again and they returned to the bookstore, they saw that Paul had picked some books off the shelves and was flipping back and forth between an iPad and the books.

"Did you find the online reviews helpful?" Sarah asked.

"Sure. But I have to read the book to find out what happens," Paul said. He looked frustrated.

"I'll buy you a couple of books to get you started," Avery said. "But you have to pick the two you like."

"And we have a special on this week: buy two, get the third free. So, you can pick three," Sarah said with a wink at Avery.

"Gee, that's great!" Paul said.

"And if you come by at three on Saturdays we have story-time readings from the Tolkien novels," Sarah added. "Each week we take a particular episode and try to bring it to life with different readers reading different characters. It's like watching a play."

Paul's eyes widened. "Who plays Gandalf?"

"Well," Sarah teased, "I'm known to wear a long beard and deepen my voice on occasion." She had deepened her voice as she spoke, and Paul's eyes widened again.

A couple of customers came into the shop, and Sarah excused herself to attend to them.

"Grandpa, these new iPads are really super," Paul said, thumbing through the various apps on the tablet.

"I thought your dad would have bought you the latest version by now."

"I asked him, because the old one was so messed up with the blood and all. But he refused. Said we have to manage with what we have, now that Mom's gone."

Damian? Manage? Since when had that word shown up in his indulged son's vocabulary? Perhaps Damian was growing up after all! Loss shaped character better than success.

"Well, you can always come in here if you want to upgrade your iPad experience. Might be good to get you out and in front of people."

"I wonder whether I could work here?"

"We'll have to ask the boss—when you're old enough, that is."

Paul grinned and returned to his new toy.

"Did you ever get in touch with Brian?" Sarah was back from serving her customers.

Avery squinted and remembered the burly birthday boy who had been proud to be thirty-five. "Oh. . .no. Another of the balls I dropped after the fire. But I'll call him. I have his card."

"It may be inconsequential now. Last I spoke to Brian, he mentioned that they were putting a hold on the class action suit until they had something concrete to go on. That's why I wondered whether his decision had been made *after* he had spoken to you."

"No. And I have very little to add on that subject. But let's not talk business now. I've been rather self-absorbed since the election and all. And I'm sorry. I'm surprised you didn't give me the boot. I'm told they fire people rather liberally these days, often via email."

"Tacky."

"Tacky indeed. As soon as Paul's off my hands, I'd like to arrange dinner. And I'd like it to be better than the last one."

"I'd like that very much too."

The doorbell tinkled, and more customers came into the store, polluting the atmosphere with foreign vibes. The spell was broken. But not before Avery felt the surge of desire in him reciprocated by her briefly in the way she touched him gently on the forearm.

Chapter 18

The house, in the eastern part of Toronto, was run down. It stood on a narrow, tree-lined street of similar houses where poor European migrants had once settled. The tall towers, encroaching on all sides since the building boom had exploded in the city, meant that these dilapidated semi-detached homes could sell for over half a million dollars apiece. Avery wondered why his well-maintained house in the suburbs, double the size of one of these aging ruins, was only half that in value. And, as for his cottage…ah, well. He certainly wasn't going to make his fortune in real-estate any more, that was for sure.

There was no doorbell or knocker; he pulled the creaky screen door aside and pounded on the faded green front door. It took nearly five minutes before it opened, although he heard movement inside way before that, as if someone had checked through the peephole and agonized over whether to admit this visitor. The figure who stood before him made him step back, startled.

Olga Beckmeyer had aged twenty years since he had last seen her, and she was bald. She leaned on a cane and smiled through loose jowls as if she had forgotten to insert her dentures before coming to the door. She was dressed in a housecoat that was threatening to fall off her skinny frame.

"Come in." She moved aside, and he stepped into the smell of stale cooking, mouldy cheese, and cigarettes. She hobbled past him while he stepped out of his shoes at the entrance. The tiny living room she ushered him into was piled with newspapers and books—a larger replica of her former work cube at Sand. A black cat nibbled on a bowl of pet food in the centre. "Don't mind Libby. She's too old to move these days, like me."

Avery moved a pile of papers aside and sat on an armchair. Olga sat opposite him in a similar chair that was clear of papers, her regular perch it appeared, facing the TV. It was the only modern fixture in the room, an HD forty-eight-inch-screen device. A laptop lay open on the side table by her chair. She pulled a lever that raised the footrest and pointed proudly at the TV. "A gift to myself for my retirement. I sleep in here most days."

"I hope I'm not stressing you out."

"No. I'll sleep after we finish this business."

"I see that you're smoking less now?" He looked at an ashtray beside her that had only a single butt in it. Olga's ashtrays had always been overflowing.

"Doctor's orders. But I sneak in one from time to time. Does the smoke bother you?"

"It's been a long time since I've been inside a smoking room."

"Open that window. It's kind of jammed and I'm too weak to open or close it these days."

Glad for the invitation to get some fresh air into the room, he rose and went to the window. He had to wrestle with the catch and strain to lift, because the metal sash had rusted right into the frame. The cool air was immediately refreshing, and he took several deep breaths before returning to his seat.

Olga leaned over, picked up an envelope that was lying next to the laptop, and tossed it at him. "Read this. Then we will talk." She settled back in her chair and closed her eyes.

The envelope had been opened and reopened many times and was quite worn. The postmark was from a month ago. A handwritten letter and some printouts on dot-matrix paper lay inside. Avery started with the letter.

Dear Olga,

You are the only person to whom I can send this letter. You are the only person left in the firm who has not moved house many times, and therefore, you were easy to track down. You are also the person who can use what I am sending you to correct the wrongs that have been done. For I knew how much you hated your job. I saw it in your face, in the way your hands moved, the day you had to sever me from the firm. I know how much you hated Martin Brock and Norman Samuels although you were their trusted hatchet man, or woman.

I ran the clinical trials for Depo-Gen, as you may recall, the generic replacement for Depo-Med. We were on an accelerated clinical trial for Depo-Gen, as Samuels and Brock were anxious to get it to market before the competition caught up. We altered some of the non-essential components to differentiate Depo-Gen from the proprietary version. We also cut corners, which I opposed, but I was overruled by my bosses. As you know, clinical trials mean nothing when it comes to measuring longer term effects. Less than ten percent of adverse reactions get reported by the time you get to the last phase of the trial, and the sample size is in the thousands of users by then. But I had my doubts and kept the names and addresses of the entire subset of trial volunteers.

Samuels and Brock hated the objections I raised at every stage of the process, and as soon as the drug had cleared its last regulatory hurdle, they sent you in to see me. The package was generous and I was weak, so I took it, partly to continue with my family tradition of beekeeping, which had been rudely interrupted by the Second World War. Brock knew my weakness and exploited it. I needed the time and focus for beekeeping, and also a generous income to support me while I indulged in this tradition of ours.

But I kept my own score on the test volunteers. Their deaths started occurring around the five-year mark following their introduction to the drug. When I investigated causes of death, in ninety-five percent of the cases it was lung cancer. And the cause did not respect age, for the deaths occurred in people as young as thirty-five to as old as sixty-five.

I have attached a graph that shows the trend line of the deaths by year, and a pie chart that splits out the causes. The original results of the clinical trials are also with me, as I smuggled home soft copies on a floppy disc when we were in the trial stage – there are a couple of boxes of the material. The results that were provided to the regulators were altered by me, at the directive of Samuels and Brock. Well, not actually altered, but "positioned," as they called it.

I know that I signed confidentiality papers as part of my exit from the firm, but now I am unable to keep quiet anymore. I am eighty-five years old and don't have much longer to live. I have enjoyed ten years of beekeeping, and the severance money has been well spent. Now is the time for reparations.

I am reluctant to go to the press myself because they may think I am a doddering old fool, someone with a grudge, or someone trying to make a buck. I don't need any bucks for this. Besides, I hate publicity, although I understand that this revelation will not be paparazzi-free. You know the authorities we dealt with, and you are in touch with the pharmaceutical industry. Please let me know how we should go about righting this wrong. I await your urgent answer.

Sincerely,

Hank Smith (my real name was Heinrich Schmidt but my parents changed it after we were taunted upon arrival in Canada for being Nazis – funny, eh?)

When Avery folded the letter, there were tears in his eyes. Pat would have been on that graph had she volunteered for the trials. As it was, she had developed her cancer roughly five years after she started using Depo-Gen.

"We are savages, aren't we?" Olga had opened her eyes and was studying him.

"Some of us are."

"No, we *all* are, in our different ways." She was leaning forward now, and her dilated pupils and shiny scalp gave her a menacing look. "Do you know what I did when I got around to reading Hank's letter? I got greedy. I phoned Brock, told him what evidence I had, and demanded more money for my severance. My cancer treatments had kyboshed my retirement plans. They've also addled my mind."

"That was silly. You could have sold this house if you needed money and moved into an apartment in the suburbs. When did you call him?"

"Two days ago. I think. I can't recall, I sleep most of the time."

"And?"

"Wait. Now I remember. It was right before I emailed you. In fact, it was because of my conversation with him that I emailed you."

"What did he say?"

"He said he'd see what he could do. But you know, the mind plays tricks when you're alone, and it's not just the effect of chemo. I didn't trust him then and I don't trust him now, especially after my phone call. I collected secrets on him when I was at Sand, for my protection. They were mostly about his philandering with employees—your girl Barbara was one of them—betcha didn't know, eh?"

"I found out. Recently."

"But this story, about the Depo-Gen, this was big, and I wanted to milk him for every penny his black soul would cough up. But I think I made a mistake. There will be no money coming from him."

"You've given him time to prepare a 'positioning statement' before carrying out your threat."

"That's why I want you to take this letter and follow up with Hank. I'm too sick to do anything more."

"Why me?"

"Because of all the people next to Hank whom I had to let go, and who hated Brock, you are it." She slumped back on the chair, spent from her burst of manic energy.

Avery folded the letter and put it in his jacket pocket. He was secretly excited. He had been waiting for an opportunity to get back into the game, his second chance, and it had arrived from the most unexpected quarter.

"I'll see what I can do. You sit back and get some rest. And don't contact Brock again, unless he comes back to you with an offer. And then I suggest you don't accept his offer. That would be complicity."

"Yes, I acted in a moment of weakness. Can you see yourself out? I think I need to take a nap."

"Yes. Goodbye, Olga."

Back in his car parked opposite the house, Avery read the letter again. This time his hands trembled when the enormity of what he held began to unfold. His whole career had been a fraud, working for people like this. There was no phone number for Hank Smith, only an address on Vancouver Island. Two boxes of material—that would mean a trip out there to pick up the boxes. Paul was still with him, reading his new books purchased from Brook's Books yesterday, and so engrossed in them that he had refused to come out with Grandpa on this trip today—good thing too! No, he couldn't fly out west until his grandson was safely back in the custody of Damian, which would be Monday at the earliest. Damn!

He released the brake and the van pulled away, just as, behind him, another car turned into the street, driven by a man in dark glasses with a pony tail, and wearing a soft leather coat.

***

Monday. A school day, because summer break was three weeks away. Avery was up at dawn making breakfast. Paul's visits motivated him to get into the kitchen and go for the full English breakfast: bacon and eggs, toast, marmalade, cereal and milk, and a can of peaches. Paul dragged himself to the table midway, the third of the Tolkien books in his hand; the other two had been devoured over the weekend.

"Wakey, wakey! Gotta look sharp for school." Avery laid a plate of eggs with two strips of bacon and a piece of toast before Paul. "Orange juice?"

"Hmm. . ." Paul was already into the book. He picked at a forkful of egg as Avery returned with the juice.

"We have forty-five minutes for breakfast, so get to it, buddy." Avery fixed his own breakfast and sat down at the dining table with his newspaper across from Paul, who had tentatively started to eat.

"Grandpa—this book is way cooler than the movies we watched yesterday."

After returning from Olga's, Avery had rented the *Lord of the Rings* trilogy on DVD, and he and Paul had spent the rest of Sunday watching them.

"Huh, that's rather surprising coming from an internet-era kid like you."

"When I read these books, I imagine a whole different set-up and scenery, and that kinda thing. In my head. And it's way cooler. The movies were like playing a video game—the same chases, the same fights, only different costumes, which we're allowed to select anyway."

"Well, I'm not much of a writer, but I read somewhere that writers only provide a few clues and it's the reader who's supposed to make up the scene in his imagination. No imagination, no scene. I was beginning to worry that kids your age had no more imagination left, because everything's now at your fingertips: when in doubt, ask Google, when you want to experience something, go to YouTube, blah de blah."

"I wish I could write a book like this. I bet it's hard."

Avery peered over his newspaper at his grandson. He couldn't believe what he was hearing. This was the kid who had tried to harm himself in a desperate plea for attention a little over a month ago, like his mother had done by surfing for boyfriends on the internet. Instead, their actions had hurt them both. But kids bounce back faster, if you give them the right trampoline, and this kid was already doing cartwheels on that trampoline. "All you need is a notebook and a pencil, for starters."

"I bet I could do it faster on my computer at home."

"Do it, then. And damn the tools."

A news article caught his eye, tucked away at the bottom of the third page, which was dedicated to news around the GTA: "Elderly cancer patient found dead in her home. Suicide assumed." The woman had been identified as one Olga Beckmeyer.

Avery read on, the egg steadily trickling off his fork. The police were investigating, as the woman was found with her head inside the gas oven in the kitchen. All the windows and doors of her semi-detached house had been locked. Her cat was also found dead nearby.

Avery had lost his appetite for breakfast by now and was trying to reread the article from the beginning when his cell phone rang.

It was Damian, and he sounded rushed. "Dad, I need another day up here. We have a number of loose ends to wrap up, and the Sand folks are demanding our submission by Thursday. Can you keep Paul until tomorrow evening? I'll be back after dinner."

"Where are you, if I may ask?"

"Muskoka. We rented one of the smaller resorts for the weekend and now we've extended it by a day. The boss is pulling out all the stops on this one."

Avery was conflicted. He was shaken by the newspaper article, unable to digest it fully, while here was Damian talking about a corporate expense account splurging on a money-making fantasy. His mind drifted back to the newspaper.

"But the window was open." The words came out of him automatically.

"Dad?"

"I opened that window! And she was too damned weak to open or close it."

"Dad. Are you talking to somebody over there?"

Avery pulled himself together when he realized that he was holding the cell phone to his ear. "Ah, yes, sorry. I was a bit distracted. Are you going through with this...this IPO thing?"

"Dad, what the hell's the matter with you? We've been over this already. This is my Big-O opportunity. Are you okay to keep Paul for another day?" Damian was sounding annoyed.

"Yeah, I'm okay. Okay. Yes, I'll keep him for another day. Call me when you get home, and I'll bring Paulie over." He hung up before Damian could ask him any more questions about his mental state. What had he agreed to do? Another day's delay in getting to Hank? With that newspaper article glaring back at him?

Composing himself—for Paul had been giving him quizzical looks during the phone conversation—Avery covered his half-eaten breakfast in plastic wrap and put it in the fridge. "That was your dad. He's delayed by a day."

"Oh, goody!" Paul took another morsel. There was still a lot of food on his plate.

"Look, buddy—we have twenty minutes. I have to make another call. You finish that food or else there'll be no more books for a while." Avery grabbed his phone, ran into the bedroom, and shut the door. He needed help and there was only one person he could turn to.

***

"Of course, I'm okay with putting Paul up for the night. I'll find something to keep him occupied. But are you sure you want to go to the other side of the country on a hunch?" Sarah's voice was even, but her concern came through on the crackly cell phone. He had given her sketchy details about his plan.

"I have to. Something's not right. Besides, there are those two boxes that need to be brought back. I'm sure Hank wouldn't entrust them to a courier, or else he'd have done that by now."

"What if the boy's mother finds out? Him staying with you is bad enough, but with me? A complete stranger?"

"It's a chance we have to take. Damian must not know either. I'll be back on the red eye tomorrow morning."

"This is about you, isn't it, Avery? It's not about Pat or the others who have died, or about Hank either. It's about you."

He didn't know how to answer that. Instead, his voice roughened. "Will you keep the boy? Pick him up after school today?"

161

"Yes, I will. Come back safe."

"Thanks!"

He disconnected and ran back into the dining room. "Okay, time's up, and there's a change of plans. You're staying at Sarah's house tonight. She drives a white Honda and will pick you up after school today. I'll write down her contact details for you in the van. I have an urgent business trip to make. I'll be back to pick you up from school tomorrow afternoon, in time for your dad's arrival."

Paul looked up. "Does that mean I get to go to the bookshop again?" The gleam in his eye said he had escaped Grandpa's rule about finishing food in order to earn more books.

"I'll let Sarah decide that." Avery looked down at Paul's half-eaten plate and almost-finished book. "And I'll forgive you your moth-eaten breakfast today providing you don't breathe a word of this...excursion... to either your mother or your father."

"Scout's honour, Grandpa! Hey, you didn't finish your breakfast either."

"Smart-ass! Now let's get a move on. I've got a plane to catch."

Chapter 19

Wolfgang Sauer stood in the prow of the ferry arriving in Nanaimo. He felt the breeze on his shaved scalp, partly covered with a Mariners baseball cap. It was a warm day, sunny, and picnickers from the mainland were crowded on board the vessel, anxiously looking forward to a day ahead of hiking, exploring, and partying. Despite it being a Monday, people in this part of the world didn't seem to work. Or maybe they were tourists, like him.

He stood in the midst of the chattering travellers, anonymous, seemingly another picnicker himself, if one were to judge from his backpack, black windbreaker, and blue denim jeans. He had needed a new look for this job. He was attached to the ponytail, which he'd shed, but it would grow back in a few months.

He eyed the dark-haired woman leaning over the rail. She looked to be in her twenties, dressed in a sleeveless top and jean shorts that hugged her curvaceous figure. His cock stirred as he watched her stretch languorously, thrusting out her breasts as she inhaled and exhaled the cool air of the Georgia Strait. He'd like to have a piece of that. But he couldn't keep his women for long; the nature of his work demanded anonymity, no attachments, and only infrequent couplings with prostitutes who knew how to please and not ask questions.

As the ferry rounded the last island and turned towards the Nanaimo harbour, his thoughts went back to the previous day. The old woman had been easy. She was snoring on her recliner when he had silently let himself into the house. She barely struggled when he held the cushion down on her face. Only the fat old cat meowed, sensing something wrong, yet it had been too weak or too lazy to do anything about it. The draft of air from the open window playing on his cheek had alerted him to check and close all doors and windows before leaving the house. Photographs on the walls had revealed enough to indicate she was of Jewish heritage. Good. That gave him the reason to hate her. Now he could finish the job off in style. He carried her limp body over to the kitchen and opened the oven door. . .

The ferry docked with a soft bump against the pier. He scanned the dock for a taxi stand; he only had an address, a hamlet somewhere inland. Sauer came down the gangway surrounded by the other passengers, then slowly veered off from them upon hitting Front Street. The dark-haired woman disappeared down an alley, like all of the women who had temporarily entered his life and departed; she had not given him a glance. A taxi cruised by, and he hailed it. He gave the address and said, "Drop me off at the crossroad."

"Tourist?" The friendly cabbie enquired. "We get many Germans in the summer."

Damn the accent! Schwarzenegger was still being called a German although he was from Austria and had been governor of California and the star of several Hollywood movies for decades.

"American," he replied. The cabbie frowned.

"Hiking?"

Sauer was taking a dislike to this cabbie. *Maybe I should kill him also.* He sucked in a deep breath and remained silent. The cabby gave him a nervous look in the rear-view mirror and focused on his driving. They didn't speak again for the rest of the journey.

The hamlet lay at the crossing of two roads on top of a hill, its only signs of commerce a general store, a gas station, and a pharmacy. Houses dotted the hills above and below the crossing, spaced far apart from each other and separated by redwoods, oak, and pine. He paid off the cabbie, added a generous tip hoping the man would think kindly of him, and began to walk downhill. When the taxi passed him heading back to Nanaimo, he paused until the vehicle was out of sight, then reversed direction.

This new target, Hank Smith—obviously an Anglicization, for the man was born in Germany—was a curiosity. He was also Jewish like the old woman, but he was a brilliant scientist, responsible for many inventions. Why did people want him dead?

It was easy for Wolfgang to hate Jews. Grandfather Sauer, a prominent lawyer, committed suicide in front of Wolfgang's ten-year old father, Klaus, rather than face the Nuremberg trials for war crimes. Father Klaus had never grown up quite right after that traumatic incident, running through a series of relationships and dead-end jobs before ending up as a clerk in a nameless government department, and siring Wolfgang off a prostitute. When the woman dumped the child on Klaus's doorstep, the court ordered him to care for young Wolfgang because the father had a regular income, unlike the mother. Klaus sought relief by inflicting regular canings on his only son, issued with manic urgency: "You will hate the Jewish bastards who brought ruin to our family." The intense beatings trained young Wolfgang to remove his mind to another place during the torture, a place where he could hate the people who had caused his father to resort to such cruelty. By the time he was thirteen, Wolfgang was plotting to kill his father, a mercy killing, he believed, for it would relieve Klaus, and him, of pain. Fortunately, Klaus blew his brains out with Grandfather's Sauer's Mauser—the same weapon that had ended the elder Sauer's life—on Wolfgang's fourteenth birthday. Wolfgang Sauer became a ward of the state. A brief stint in the army did not abate his hate for those who had moulded his life. In fact, it amplified and morphed into a full-time career when he killed his first Jew at the age of twenty-one: a contract killing where the body was never discovered, dumped into a building site that received a fresh layer of concrete the following day. The boost of validation from that first attempt at "hitting back" had felt like an aphrodisiac.

But this scientist intrigued him. Hank Smith would be the first Jew of eminence he had been tasked to scrub out. His victims had usually been merchants, bankers, pro-Israel backers, or sycophantic puppets who supported big business. Smith was someone who had contributed to saving lives. Or had he?

The climb uphill left him winded and sweating. He was fifty now, and physical exertion was starting to bother him. He would need a different job soon. He should buy a quiet little pub in Bavaria and settle down with a piece of flesh like that dark-haired woman, and not have to pay for sex anymore. And yet the thrill of the kill would gnaw at him. He needed to kill to live, and he needed to outwit the authorities at every turn, those authorities who had forced his grandfather and father to commit suicide and had dictated life to him through foster homes and other sterile state institutions. He'd been killing for too long, without being caught; it was his drug of necessity, not of choice.

He passed the address: a long driveway running through a wooded entrance. He doubled back when there were no vehicles or passers-by in sight. The property was well cared for, the fence unbroken, the undergrowth cleared, and no potholes in the gravel. German efficiency? Or Jewish diligence? Both. It bothered Sauer that this scientist embodied the best of Germany in his résumé and in his lifestyle.

He stepped behind a bush, pulled out the Walther from his backpack, fixed the silencer onto it, and slid the weapon into his waistband, underneath the windbreaker. Guns were not his preferred method of operation—too messy, and they raised too many questions—but it was his backup, in case things didn't go the way he had planned.

He rounded a bend and came upon the house, a single-storey, wooden A-frame structure with a brown lacquer finish and a "Sold" sign below the porch steps. A wing projecting from the left was a later addition to the original; it had fresher white siding. A triangular pile of logs, recently cut, evident by the woodchips strewn around, was stacked by the fence at the far end under an oak tree, and a new strand of barbed wire ran between the fence posts closest to the pile.

When he went around the side of the house, he saw the white boxes, and the figure in the hat, veil, and body suit walking among them.

***

Hank straightened up after placing the last log on the woodpile. He hadn't expected to chop it all up today, but that had been one mighty branch that had fallen in last week's rainstorm, and he had been determined to get it out of the way. And the new strand of barbed wire was a dead giveaway of what had happened, and could happen again, if more of that tree came down in the next storm. But he was past worrying about yard maintenance—let the new owner figure it out.

He was too tired to haul the wood into the shed today, having swung mightily with the axe for a couple of hours. Tomorrow, Bob would bring his dolly over and help him. He hadn't been into the store for his newspaper yet, either. Perhaps later this evening.

Hank picked up the axe and began to head indoors, then glanced towards the hives and couldn't resist going over. The bees were his domain; not even Bob was allowed to go near them nor assist with the annual honey harvest. He lay the axe down by the lever unit, donned his suit, hat, and veil lying on the grass nearby, and walked among the boxes, touching their covers with affection, lifting an occasional lid to hear the humming, and watch the writhing mass in its treacly sludge, working, working, always working, like he had done all his life. There was some work remaining here: removing the honey-coated frames from the supers for storage in the shack to be subsequently worked on by the new owner; withdrawing the excluder panels to release the queen bees from their brood chambers into the supers to mix with the workers and the drones in each of the hives. Robbed of their honey, the bees would be ready to leave with their queens and colonize elsewhere. But he would leave this work for just before his departure from the island, so that the honey remained fresh, with the bees only recently introduced to a new state of agitation. And then his beloved honeybees would be gifted to the world. The ceremonious act of pulling the lever and releasing them would be his moment of glory, and he had dreamed about it constantly. Walking down the line of boxes, his hand caressed the handle of the lever system that he had constructed, imagining the day when he would actually pull it. *It won't be long...*

His one worry now was the lack of response to his letter. It had taken too long. Was Olga Beckmeyer the right one to have sent it to? But who else could he have trusted? There was that VP of Marketing chap...what was his name...Mann? Mann had opposed generics at the time, but Hank had left Sand so long ago, he did not know if allegiances had changed and hearts won over by those clever spinmeisters, Brock and Samuels.

They must come soon....

Then he turned around and saw the man in the baseball cap coming around the side of the house. *They are here...*

***

Sauer watched the veiled figure remove his headgear and wave, a smile on his face, as if he had been expected. The old man looked positively pleased to see him. *I'm having difficulty hating him.*

When Sauer was within a couple of feet from the last white box in the line, the old man called out from the other end, "What took you so long?"

This guy is wütend! Sauer decided to play with him. "Olga took a little time to deal with."

"She sure took her damned time."

Sauer raised his eyebrows this time. Was he hearing this guy right?

Without any sign that he might be humouring the visitor, the old man continued. "I see you are also from Germany?"

"Munchen."

"Berlin for me. I don't get to practise my German often." The old man had lapsed into speaking German.

Sauer responded, also in his native tongue, relieved at not having to think in one language and translate into another. "Olga died peacefully in the end."

168

The old man's eyebrows knit in a puzzled frown with disappointment showing at the edges. "She's dead? I know she suffered from cancer once, long ago. Do you have a message from her?"

Sauer was having difficulty with his victim's naïveté. *He is not so smart after all, just an eccentric old duffer.* "No message." He slid his hands under his windcheater.

"Are you with the press?"

"No."

Alarm gripped the old man's features. "Then who are you?"

Sauer withdrew the gun. It usually provided all the answers his victims needed to know. Hank Smith exhaled and his frame seemed to shrink inside the bee suit. "Brock? I didn't think he'd go this far."

Sauer pointed with the gun towards the house. "We are going indoors. I believe you have some papers for me."

The old man held his ground. "Why would you hurt a fellow German?"

"You are a Jew."

"I am German, first and foremost."

"My grandfather and father died because of scum like you." Sauer was working himself up to hate this man.

"So, you are a Nazi then. Or the descendant of one."

"We were assumed guilty when the war ended. The victors are always innocent, the vanquished are the guilty."

"That is not how we saw it when our family business was destroyed by you Nazis, and my parents were sent to Belsen. I was smuggled out to England, from where I was able to get to Canada. I am the only survivor of my entire family. We were guilty without knowing why. I always wanted to kill myself a Nazi."

"Well, dream on, old man. Are you going to tell me where the papers are or do I shoot you right here?"

The old man's shoulders drooped and his voice dropped to a whisper. "Okay, I will give you the papers…"

***

The hate in his heart gushed, choking him, and he coughed. Here was the reason for his life's emptiness, standing in front of him, the accursed Nazi—this one was too young, neo-Nazi then— the symbol of his family's loss, the impetus to his years spent trying to find a home, the consigner of the solitary life that had been his lot, and the robber of his ability to form lasting relationships. Oh, if he were twenty years younger.

That this steely-eyed stranger would take him into the house and murder him, he was certain. And not a soul would know. His self-sought isolation was now his undoing. And once he stepped away from this spot, his bees would never be set free. They would work themselves to death and perish in their hives, like the Jews of Europe who suffocated in the gas chambers. No, he could not let that happen. Over his dead body, he wouldn't.

He had been gripping the lever handle unconsciously as they talked. Now he felt its warmed metal inside his sweaty palm. It wouldn't be on Canada Day, after all. Nothing said that it couldn't be now. But the honey was still in the hives and the queens were trapped in their brood chambers; if released now, the worker bees would return.

But for him, it was now or never. He pulled the handle.

***

When the lids of the boxes snapped open in unison with a reverberating shudder that rocked the hives, Sauer was taken aback by its precision and suddenness. In reflex, he trained the gun at the old man who was a harmless distance away, hanging onto the lever that had released the covers. Sauer eased back. *No need to change plans yet. No need for the gun yet. Don't panic.*

An angry buzzing that increased in volume was followed by a furious scurrying, and thin black smoke-like clouds rose from inside the wide-open hives.

Smith had put his veil back on and turned his back on Sauer, and was looking out over the valley with his hands raised like Moses before the

170

Promised Land, commanding in a booming voice, "Go, my dears. Go and pollinate, and may you never be eradicated from this planet."

The bees were starting to spread, to widen their area of activity, and to thicken as more and more of them emerged from their boxes. The sky was starting to darken with this explosion of creator bees, the antidote to the Biblical plague of predator locusts. A sickly-sweet smell— overripe bananas—wafted from the boxes in the wake of the bees. Sauer stood mesmerized. He had never seen anything like this. In that instant of release, Sauer perceived that there was something that bonded him with his victim: they were both loners, one creating, the other destroying, while the rest of the world lay before them, blissfully unaware of these solitary men's efforts. He was deadlocked between wanting to hate this man and giving in to the impulse to respect him.

A sharp jab of pain above his right eye, followed by a furious buzzing around him, awoke him to the fact that he was exposed and uncovered. Sauer waved his hands in front of his face, but he was being stung from all sides. He seemed to have become encased in bees while he had his attention diverted on Smith. He tried to run backwards, but tripped and fell. His eyes began tearing rapidly and his face started swelling up. The pain was excruciating. The bees were attacking him from all angles; they had crept down his windbreaker and were stinging him on the chest and deeper down. He had never been stung by a bee in his life, and this crippling pain was worse than been shot by a gun—which had happened to him on more than one occasion. Now he hated this Jew bastard for the bee stings. Now he had the reason to kill, and he was going to kill Smith. He swivelled on the grass trying to find his target, but his vision was blurred. His face was ballooning by the second, forcing his eyelids to narrow into slits and close up. All that his senses registered were the buzzing and the numbing pain.

Then he made out a veiled figure advancing, like an angel of death with something that resembled a scythe in its hands—the Grim Reaper, as his conscience had always warned, who would come for him one day no matter how many times he cheated the authorities. He fired, but the figure kept advancing. Missed. He took aim again, keeping his gun in the shadow of the apparition that was now almost upon him. He pulled the trigger again, just as the axe came crashing down on his neck.

Chapter 20

Sarah parked her white Honda in the school lot and watched the children stream out of the public primary school. Tousled, tired, ebullient, shrieking, quiet—a mix of emotions aroused by being caged up for a day in a classroom. Some streamed into the row of school buses lined up along the service road, others walked towards cars in designated parking spots, and still others dispersed in either direction along the street opposite the school, towards homes in the neighbourhood.

She saw Paul immediately, standing tentatively outside the school building, looking around, seemingly lost compared to his mates. She remembered Avery telling her that this child had been enrolled in a private school until last year, but when the marriage got into trouble and financial woes mounted, he had been yanked out and put into public school to tough it out with the rest of Canada's middle class. A lot for this kid to bear, along with the impending family split. Looking at him now, Sarah saw that Paul did not display the confidence he had radiated at the bookshop shop the other day. But on that occasion, he had been with his grandfather, the only person he could rely on.

I can't disappoint him.

She got out of the car and waved to him. "Hi Paul, over here."

Seeing her, he immediately broke into a grin and ran over.

"Get in the front seat and buckle up. You can tell me all about school as we drive over to my place."

His step suddenly slowed as he neared. He was looking over her shoulder. Then he came to a complete stop, a conflicted look of disappointment and alarm on his face. Sarah had been so intent on the boy that she hadn't been aware of her surroundings. When a figure came up from behind her, rushed over, and grabbed Paul by the arm, she gasped.

The woman, a redhead in an elegant mauve fall coat and matching shoes, flashed flaming green eyes. "Lay off my child. Who are you?"

The tumblers clicked. "I'm Sarah."

"You're a bit old to be Damian's girlfriend."

"I'm not. I'm Avery's friend."

"Huh, this gets deeper. Are you kidnapping my son?"

Sarah sighed. This was going to be complicated. How to explain? She noticed that the redhead—she couldn't remember the boy's mother's name—was squeezing Paul's arm so tightly he was wincing, tears hovering in the corners of his eyes.

"Why don't you let go of Paul. I can explain all this."

"You'd better. And it had better be good, or I'm calling the police." The woman fished out her cell phone with her now freed hand. Paul scampered over to the passenger side of the Honda and leaned against the door, as if he was trying to put the car between himself and his mother.

Sarah took a deep breath. "I was going to look after Paul for the night—"

"You!" The woman interrupted. "Who the hell are you to do that? His father should be looking after him. Where *is* his father?"

"Damian was detained out of town on business."

"As usual! At the very least, I would have not been surprised to see Paul's grandfather here, even though he has no business looking after Paul."

"Avery too was called away on an urgent matter. Both of them will be returning tomorrow. I stepped into help."

"This is ridiculous. They both bugger off and entrust my child to a stranger? And they don't bother to tell me? Shouldn't a mother look after her child?"

Paul suddenly shrieked from behind Sarah. "But you left us. You left me!"

The redhead looked like she had been slapped. Her fiery gaze shifted to the boy cowering behind the car.

"You...ungrateful...wretch!"

At which point, Paul burst out crying. Sarah rushed over to the boy and put her arms around him. She could feel his shuddering and sobbing—a mixture of anger and sadness.

She looked at the other woman imploringly. "Can we dial this down? If the school authorities see us carrying on like this, we could all be in trouble. Let's put Paul into my car, or into yours if you came in one, wherever he'll feel safe and comfortable, and let's go over to that bench and talk this over like civilized people."

"I don't want to go with Mom. I want to go with you." Paul was sobbing.

Sarah shrugged. *Now what?*

Paul's reluctance to go with his mother was having an effect. The redhead looked near to tears.

"Please..." Sarah entreated. "Let's talk."

The woman took a deep breath as if to hold back her tears, strode over to the bench located where the playground bordered the parking lot, and sat down. She kept her gaze on Sarah and Paul all the time.

Sarah opened the passenger side door of her car, asked Paul to get in, and put his seat belt on. The boy meekly complied. He immediately fished out an iPad from his satchel and started playing a video game as if to blot out the world. "I'll be back shortly," Sarah told him, closing the car door.

She walked over to the park bench. The red-headed woman was crying. Her sobs resembled Paul's but also sounded laced with regret.

"Sorry, I don't know your name. I only know that you're Paul's mother."

"I'm Sylvana."

"Thank you. Sylvana, if Paul is willing, I have no problem if he goes with you. I'll just need to let Avery know. But I think the boy is quite upset right now. It might be best if I keep him for the night until he settles down. I will, of course, give you all my contact details so you'll know where he is and how he's faring at all times that he is with me."

"This is highly irregular."

"Aren't our lives also irregular when compared to the norm?"

"I wanted so much for us. For Paul."

Sarah reached out and took Sylvana's hand. It was hard, with taut muscles. Athletic. Or neurotic.

"Divorce is not easy for a ten-year-old. His whole world is being upended."

"You think mine isn't?"

"But you don't have to do it. Leaving the marriage was your choice."

"Living with Damian is impossible. He's never around."

"Perhaps he may be feeling that if he doesn't put in the hours, all the things you have and desire would not be possible. Have you tried downscaling, or counselling? I did both after my husband died. It was wonderful having fewer things to care about, although I still have a bookshop that struggles to keep its head up. One day I'll give that one up too."

"You sound like my mother. But my father would be ashamed of me. Thank God he's dead."

"Living to please ghosts is not an ideal state of being."

Sylvana abruptly rose. "Paul can go with you. If he doesn't want me, I don't want him."

Sarah reached into her pocket and pulled out a business card. She fished out a pen and scribbled her home address and phone numbers, and her car licence plate as well. "Here's how to reach me."

Sylvana took the card without even looking at it, turned on her heel, and crossed the parking lot towards a silver SUV. She got in and drove off without even a glance towards Sarah or Paul.

Chapter 21

Avery's flight got into Vancouver at 3 p.m. Pacific time. He had booked himself on the red-eye back to Toronto, leaving before midnight, and hoped that he would be able to conclude his business with Hank Smith well in time. He took a taxi from the airport to the ferry terminal and read his email and texts on his BlackBerry en route.

There was a text from Sarah: *Picked up Paul from school. We had a visit to the bookshop followed by an interesting dinner at McDonald's. Haven't been there in years. Heading home now. Not sure what we will do together, but we will play it by ear. Paul is good training for me for when my grandchildren get older. Hope Vancouver is fine. Be safe.*

There was an email from Barbara: *Hi Avery. Thanks for writing. I guess my anger has now dissipated and I am able to think clearly. You are right. We were not intended to cross the lines we had set for ourselves and maintained for years. I took up the opportunity to contact Mark Preston. We are meeting tomorrow morning. Will keep you posted. Thanks!*

This summed up the women in his life. Strangely, since the fire, he had not given much thought to Pat. Perhaps he had begun the act of closure when he started stowing her things away in the basement. Besides, he had been so busy in the act of his own recovery during the last month, in regaining lost ground, in being grounded in the present, that he'd had no time to dwell on the past. Was this a sign that he was finally moving on? But then, why was he here on the West Coast chasing an elusive scientist with a secret? "It's about you, isn't it?" Sarah's words came back to him. Yes, this wasn't about Pat, this was about putting closure to his *career interruptus.*

On the packed ferry, excited chatter and assorted smells of food, perfume, and sweat wafted over him in the confines of the cabin. Those out on deck were turning darker shades of tan between departing the mainland and arriving on the island.

Well's Junction, the location on Hank's mailing address, was simply an intersection of two roads. He asked the taxi driver to drop him off at the crossing and stepped into the general store on the northeast corner to get directions. The woman behind the counter greeted him with a smile, and it widened when she saw the address on the old envelope he slipped her.

"Oh, that's Hank's place. He's up the hill from us. Fifth property as you head north. Are you a family member of Hank's?"

"An old colleague from out east."

"We. . .my husband and I. . ." she pointed to a man in overalls who was stacking merchandise on shelves, ". . .we kind of look after Hank. But he's leaving."

"Leaving?"

"You'll see the big 'Sold' sign outside his house. He's heading back east." She cast her gaze down at the counter and sighed.

"Well, I'd better get to him before he leaves."

"Oh, no—that's not until the end of this month, I believe. We don't know why he's leaving. He'll miss his bees."

"It must get pretty lonely up there for him. He's not a young man anymore."

She nodded. "Bob and I do what we can for him. But he's very private. He gets a bit winded once in a while, especially when he has to climb the hill and that. Tell him Lydia says hi."

"I will."

Buying a bottle of mineral water to quench his thirst, Avery said goodbye to the couple and continued his journey. He too was winded by the time he got to the fifth mailbox and could imagine how tough it must be for Hank these days. He walked down the long driveway, which seemed to run through a thick copse of trees cleared of underbrush— *Hank must do a lot of work to maintain this place, or else he must pay a lot to get it done.*

The house was bathed in soft evening sunshine, and the vista of surrounding trees, tall and protective, the ocean in the distance, the chirping of birds, and the gentle breeze that brushed his face made him realize why people gave up the struggle back east to come out to this haven of peace. It wasn't all about building real-estate nest eggs, for there was something to be said about stepping off the grid. He had tried to do that himself with his cottage…and…although right now he didn't want to dwell on *that* disaster, he seemed to be getting constant reminders of it. But the "Sold" sign on Hank's driveway stoked the thought of other transitions: the "For Sale" sign on Damian's property, and the "Fire Damage" sign on his own. It was as if the gods were conspiring to wipe out his past and start him on a new course, and that course had begun on the day he had been introduced to Martin Brock in Norman Samuels's office.

There was no doorbell or knocker. He pounded on the door and waited. After a couple of minutes, hearing with no movement inside, he tried the doorknob and found the door unlocked. A shiver crept down his spine. He tried to brush it off, reminding himself that in this isolated part of the island, people didn't need to lock their doors, let alone have locks on them.

"Anybody home?" he called from inside the threshold.

He was met with only his echoing voice followed by silence. With a rapidly beating heart, he stepped further into the house. The living room with its giant fireplace, now cleaned out and awaiting the next heating season, welcomed him. The house was tidy, not a single object askew, everything parallel or at right angles to each other, a mathematician's house, although everything in it was old. This A-frame area was dark, with heavy rugs and furniture, and lots of pictures on the walls. He made out faded sepia photographs taken in Germany in the early part of the twentieth century. There was none from Hank's life in Canada. Avery walked into the newer, better-illuminated section of the house, where a computer sat on a work desk attached to a dot-matrix printer. On the desk were sketches of some kind of lever and pulley system. Bookshelves ran around the walls. A cardboard box on the floor had more books in them, as if someone was unpacking, or packing to leave. He scanned the titles.

In the corporate world, people did not discuss books, unless it was the latest, faddish business book. He remembered having a discussion with colleagues once during an off-site meeting about *In Search of Excellence,* which had recently hit the best-seller lists. Here, there were titles on literature, science, art, philosophy, politics, and beekeeping. It was strange, Avery thought, that when one was released from the corporate yoke, the mind blossomed, grabbing for knowledge denied it due to the exigencies of time, work, and political correctness. One title caught his attention: *The Art of Beekeeping* by Hans Friedrich Schmidt, translated from German into English by one Hank Smith. Avery shook his head; you never knew what talent lurked in the colleague who sat in the cubicle next to you.

This new wing had French doors that faced out onto the back garden and the ocean beyond. That's when Avery saw the white boxes. They had been obscured from his view when he had approached the house down the front driveway. *Beehives.* He glanced back at the sketches on the desk; a replica of the lever and pulley system in the diagram was connected to the row of hive boxes in the garden via spokes running from a central metal stem hung above the boxes. A spoke was connected to the lid of each box. All but a couple of the boxes had their lids open, and it looked as if the opening of the boxes had been initiated by pulling down on the large handle at one end of the row. Small bee squadrons hovered over the open boxes. *That's odd? Why are they open?*

He then saw the fallen figures in the grass, like waxworks in a deathly tableau.

"My God!"

He threw open the French windows that led to a deck, ran across it, and leapt into the back garden. He was met with the strong smell of bananas that had gone well past their "best by" date. He came across the tall man in the Mariners baseball hat first. The axe was embedded deep in the man's throat, almost severing it clean, and he held a gun in his right hand fitted with a silencer. His face was pock-marked and swollen, an unusual swelling, as if allergic to bee stings. Some bees still hovered over the body. Avery stumbled over to the next figure, lying three feet away, face up, dressed in a beekeeper costume, including the hat and veil. This man's chest was stained crimson around what looked like a bullet hole. Avery lifted the veil. An older version of Hank Smith, as he remembered the man, stared back at him through blank eyes. Both men had been dead for some time.

Avery staggered over to the boxes but ran out of steam and fell down on the grass. He realized that he too was exposed and was running the risk of being stung. But so far, he was unscathed. *Perhaps bees can differentiate between good guys and bad guys better than we humans.* More bees kept returning from various parts of the garden to the disturbed boxes, and pausing before disappearing inside.

Slowly, what had transpired in this haven of peace materialized for him. No one in the neighbourhood would have seen or heard anything given the isolation that shrouded this property. And here he was stumbling around, disturbing a crime scene. He must get help. But where to call, whom to call first? When his racing heart had eased, he fished his BlackBerry out, went back to the corpses and took photographs of them, focusing on several closeups of the man in the baseball cap. It was hard work, with bees buzzing increasingly in the background, and yet they didn't attack him like they had the dead man. Avery was at the point of retching from the strain by the time he finished photographing the scene.

Not wanting to push his luck, he retreated to the back deck, out of range of the bees, pulled up a wooden lounge chair to face the bodies, and sat thinking. He had phone calls to make. He searched inside his wallet and pulled out the card that had been idling there for over a month; Alex Mendoza wouldn't believe in his good fortune. Avery also had to call Damian, who might be putting the final wraps on the IPO about now.

But he didn't have anything to offer either of them other than Hank's letter to Olga with its accusations devoid of solid proof. The test result papers must be somewhere in this house and he had to find them before he called the police, for that was the third call he had to make before too much time elapsed.

Avery hadn't seen any boxes inside other than the one with books, and this house didn't have a basement. He stepped out of his shoes and went back indoors through the French doors in his socks, searching, including inside the bedroom and bathroom, poking around for a loft or a loose ceiling board in the newer section. Nothing. Stymied, he came out, slipped back into his shoes, and flopped on the chair again, placing his cell phone on the armrest.

The white boxes, haloed by their former buzzing occupants, stared back at him. *I am surrounded by boxes but I can't find the ones I want!*

Then he stood up and stared. All the boxes had opened and released their deadly cargo except for the two at the end closest to the lever handle; their lids were not connected with spokes to the lever system either. He ran back to the row of boxes, approaching upwind where the bees were thinnest, shivering as he passed the corpses. Reaching the first closed box, he grabbed the lid and yanked it open. He instinctively drew back, expecting a swarm of startled bees to greet him. Instead, a pile of perforated print paper in a transparent plastic bag stared back at him.

"Aha!" He pulled the lid off the second box, and it too held similar contents.

He had disturbed too much of this crime scene by now, and there would be a lot of explaining to do. And there was a red-eye flight to catch, if the police would let him. Avery rushed back to the deck and his cell phone to start making those phone calls.

***

In another part of the country, darkness had descended. Sarah sat in her corner nook reading a book after having tucked Paul into bed in the guest bedroom. They had enjoyed a fun evening together, playing with

Storyteller, a video game that allowed you to make your own story and try different combinations of characters, plot twists, and endings. Paul had come up with the weirdest combinations, which made them both laugh heartily. She hoped the stories helped him sleep better after what had transpired at school that day.

She worried about this young family. Compared to hers, which had experienced its own share of tragedy, this one was unstable at its roots. Avery did not have much to his legacy, despite how hard he had worked for it. She wished she could make things even marginally better for him.

The phone rang. She jumped up and grabbed it before it could wake Paul in the other room. This must be Avery.

It was Sylvana. Sarah's heart skipped.

"Hello, Sarah?" Sylvana sounded mellow compared to earlier. Had she been drinking?

"Yes." Sarah rushed to fill the silence on the line, scared of what might come across if she didn't stop talking. "Paul had a great time playing a video game with me. We had dinner at McDonald's—Paul had a Big Mac and a chocolate milkshake. I hope that was okay. He's sleeping quite contentedly now."

"Thank you."

"Oh, my pleasure. Paul is a lovely boy. Very bright, very curious, and unafraid to experiment with new ideas."

"No, I meant thank you for talking to me today. I knew Paul would be safe with you."

Sarah couldn't believe what she was hearing. All she could do was repeat, "Oh, my pleasure. You're most welcome."

"I thought about what you said— 'Living to please ghosts is not an ideal state of being.'"

"I'm sure my husband would have preferred me to live a chaste widow. But I didn't want to remain married to a ghost."

"Can one ever go back?"

"It depends how far off the shore you've drifted. In my case, my husband died—there was *no* going back. Your husband is still alive. And your son misses you both."

There was silence on the line, then a sob. "I need help, Sarah. Can you help me?"

Sarah took a deep breath. *This is a long shot. But heck, I've taken longer ones in my life.*

"I have an idea. . ."

Chapter 22

Martin Brock walked into Sand Pharmaceuticals's headquarters and nodded to the receptionist on the ground floor. His usual entrance would be a rushed walk into the elevator to take it to the penthouse suite, to a meeting already in progress and waiting his late but important arrival. Today he had cleared his calendar for the morning, as he wanted to work on his speech for the IPO road show. It was important to showcase his years of toil up to the corporate firmament, for people always bought the author, not the book, and it was his stellar record as CEO that would carry this deal through to success.

But today, he paused to speak to the receptionist. "Good morning, Rosie!" He knew her name, for he screened all employee hires and memorized their names, including those of the contract reception staff who serviced the building. This came in handy at employee events when he would move among the troops and single out people by first name. Made one look like a fabulous boss. The receptionist smiled and blushed, because she was not used to the president of the largest tenant in the building showering her with attention.

He took the elevator to the twenty-first floor. Sand's corporate logo adorned the wall of the suite. His personal assistant, Natalie, full bodied and efficient, fluttered her eyelashes as he entered. He had fired the older one, Norman Samuels's PA of over twenty years, because he needed young blood. Besides, Natalie was a divorcee with no children, and they played a flirtatious dance that had not extended to the bedroom yet. He kept it that way. To cross the line was to lose power. He had learned that the hard way with women like Barbara. He liked Natalie's work and her cockteasing, and that was enough. Besides, he had plenty of amusement on the online dating circuit these days.

"I have coffee going already," Natalie said, rising and rolling her hips towards the coffee machine. As she bent over to pour the beverage, he caught a glance of her cleavage through the V-neck of her blouse. She dressed for the occasion: in business suits for board meetings and external events, in low-cut, flimsy wear for when they were alone, and today was one of those days. She must pick her wardrobe according to his calendar, he thought.

"I'll have two sugars today," he said. "It's a good day. Don't put through any calls unless it's the Premier people on the IPO. They've been at it all weekend and should be done by now."

Their fingers caressed as she slid the coffee mug into his hand. She smiled coquettishly. "Call me if there is anything else you need. . .sir."

Every time Brock entered his office, he paused. This was the seat of power, and he held it. The room was large and had windows looking out on the lake from two angles. Lots of glass and light. One wall held all the trophies awarded to Sand—for innovation, community support, hospital foundation support, golf tournament sponsorships, and service club awards. The mahogany desk was the size of a car, and the plush dark leather armchair that he lost himself in daily was fit for a king. It had taken a long, hard slog to get to this office.

And very soon there would be a bigger office for him when Sand moved out to the suburbs. He had personally supervised the design of his "Office of the President & Chief Executive Officer." He had to hand it to himself, the overall rent for the new premises was a fraction of this downtown tower, but he had ended up with more space for himself. He would be able to practise his twenty-five-foot putt in his new digs.

Despite the dark side he traversed, he had managed to create and navigate the path of corporate social responsibility, which was so important to the modern corporation. There was a time for toil and a time for reflection, and today was the time for the latter, one so infrequently indulged in due to his headlong rush to the top. And a couple of very important events were about to unfold: the IPO, and news that two irritating past employees would not be interfering in his plans anymore.

He had already heard about Olga Beckmeyer from yesterday's newspapers and expected to be hearing from Sauer on the other one shortly.

He sipped his coffee and switched on his desktop computer. What to say in introducing himself to the investment community? They had to be confident in a man who treated his role as more than a job, it had to be a part of his life. But how could he tell them about the impoverished child living with his single mother, who had a penchant for drinking and picking loser boyfriends, until a scholarship delivered him? It did not pay to talk about being of the wrong pedigree in these circles. The old boys club route was better and safer in corporate Canada circles. He'd keep the rags-to-riches story for when they traded in New York later; the Yanks liked the Rocky Balboas and the Gordon Gekkos. But those formative, impoverished days had been the conditioning, the genesis that gave way to a personal philosophy of "Me first, and fuck the rest of the world."

And yet, Sauer bothered him. This was by far the farthest he'd stretched himself. And the reality is that there was no way back after taking that kind of step. *You have to keep going and enjoy the ride.* In a way, he felt relieved that he had fewer moral restraints to hold him back now. *The other side, the ruled, is made up of fodder, puppets to be manipulated and disposed of when they are no longer useful* —Phelps's words. Brock had actually done Olga a favour and saved her from a lingering death. As for Hank Smith, how many more years did he have? He'd provided Hank an escape from the nursing home and the ignominy of old age. No, he had no qualms about Olga and Hank, but he worried about Sauer.

The intercom rang. "I've got Damian Morgan from Premier Investments on the phone," Natalie's husky voice purred.

"Put him through." Brock's heartbeat increased a notch. "Damian, my boy, how are you? How'd the offsite go?"

Damian's voice sounded strained.

Perhaps they got the secretaries to do the work and boozed all weekend.

"I've got some good news and some bad news," Damian began. He seemed to be reading from a script.

"Give me the good news first."

"Well, we ploughed through the documentation and have everything ready."

"Wonderful! So, what can hold us back? What's this bad news?"

"We don't believe you should proceed with this offering. Not at this time."

"What? Are you mad, man?"

"Some…well, some new evidence has come to light that makes the timing of this event rather untimely."

"What the hell, Damian—I mean the stock market has recovered from 2008, our balance sheet and income statement are the best they've ever been in years. Have you guys gone chicken? There are other investment brokers, you know."

"I'm sorry, Martin. I'm only the messenger here, and being your interface into the investment community, I was nominated to pass on this news to you. A formal letter will be faxed to you later this morning with our decline."

"I'll sue you for damages! Do you know how much time and effort has gone into this on our side?"

"We feel the same, Mr. Brock. We spent a lot of resources on this gig too."

The transition from first name to formal name was upsetting to Brock. "I'll sue the shit out of you guys and make you the pariahs of the investment community. You are walking away from one of the best deals you'll come across in a long time. I need to speak to your boss." Brock had risen and was pacing. He pulled his tie down and flipped the top button of his shirt so hard that it broke off and rolled along his desk.

"My boss prefers to communicate in writing. We spent a lot of time and money too, Mr. Brock. But we are prepared to cut our losses at this stage rather than be completely embarrassed when the offer comes out. As my father advised me last night, saying 'no' is also an option."

Brock discovered that he had completely twisted the squeeze ball, one that he kept on his desk for periods of concentration, beyond recognition. "You can tell your father to kiss my ass."

"As a matter of fact, I believe you know him. His name is Avery Mann."

Brock stopped pacing, like he had walked into a battering ram. His breathing sounded laboured as he roared into the phone, "Mann is your father?"

"Yes, Morgan is my mother's maiden name."

"Well, fuck you and fuck your father. And I'll see you all in court."

Brock slammed the phone down before there was any comeback from the other side. He would show them. Now his blood was boiling. This was a minor setback, but those bastards at Premier Investments would be well worth going after. Suddenly it occurred to him, that despite all the anger he had expressed, he had never found out *what* had caused the PI team to change its mind.

The intercom rang again. Natalie sounded worried. She must have overheard his shouting through the door of his office. "Are you okay, Martin?"

"Yes. But I'll be better after I see our lawyers. Get them on the phone for me, will you?"

"Sure thing." Then her voice dropped a notch. "But there's this guy in the waiting area. I know you don't want to be disturbed today. He has no appointment. But he said he was calling to 'shoot the shit'—his words, not mine—as you had asked him to one night in a parking garage. He looks like he hasn't slept in a week. Gave his name as Avery Mann. Do you want to see him, or shall I send him away?"

***

Avery paced the waiting room, awaiting the return of Brock's personal assistant from the CEO's inner sanctum. Her reception towards him had been cool initially, and he blamed his appearance for that—he must have smelled bad from the blood, sweat, tears, and honey of the last twenty-four hours. His bleary eyes from lack of sleep after being stuck in the middle seat on a red-eye flight did not make him any more appealing. When he had insisted on seeing Brock, she became hostile, defensive of the man behind the mahogany doors. When he had banged his hand on the reception desk, she buzzed the boss reluctantly, only to be summoned immediately into his presence. Now, Avery waited. Boss and assistant had been in camera for ten minutes.

He couldn't believe the flurry of activity that had been precipitated by his phone calls while sitting on the back deck of Hank Smith's house the day prior: a one-way conversation with Damian during which all he had heard back was a series of "um. . .buts" until the other side of the phone had lapsed into silence; an excited Alex Mendoza who wanted more and more, even though Avery left out details of the double killing that was staring him in the face on Hank's deck and had stuck only to the concealed test results story; and when the cops arrived, an unending police statement on what had transpired after he arrived at Smith's house that afternoon. Fortunately, the couple at the general store, who had hurried to the house when the police sirens blasted the neighbourhood, were able to corroborate his statement about what time he had arrived at Well's Junction; the couple were devastated by what they saw, and the woman had to be escorted home by the police soon afterwards. After Avery's lawyer in Toronto had intervened by phone, the investigating officer let him travel back on the red-eye, as long as he reported to the RCMP in Ontario within twenty-four hours of his flight's arrival back home, and as long as he did not talk to anyone (ha ha!). The two boxes of test results were taken into the custody of the RCMP, labelled "Evidence Collection." Hank's letter to Olga still reposed in Avery's backpack, as it had not come up in the interrogation by the police.

The mahogany doors opened, and the administrative assistant stood with hands behind her back. She looked like she would need a fresh coat of makeup and a stiff drink. "Mr. Brock will see you now." As she stepped aside to let him pass, he sensed her suppressed shiver.

Brock was at his desk, the sunlight from the surrounding windows casting his features in shadow. He did not rise to greet his visitor. Avery walked in and took a seat in front of his old rival without invitation.

"I took you up on your offer."

"You've picked an inconvenient time. You have ten minutes."

"I only need three."

"You've lost thirty seconds already."

Avery pulled out his BlackBerry, flipped to the Pictures icon and pulled up the most recent one, the closeup of the dead man in the baseball hat. "Recognize this man?" He extended the phone over Brock's expansive desk.

When Brock blinked and his facade of impassivity slipped, Avery withdrew the phone and sat back in his chair. "At least you are not a psychopath—yet. You still have emotions."

"What do you want?" Brock had regained his composure, but his voice was raspy. His hands were clasped in front of him on the desk.

"Let me use my last minute to tell you this: Hank's secret is out in the open. The police are now involved. Their wheels grind slowly, but you will be hearing from them. The newspapers are close behind. Don't leave town."

"I don't know the man in that photo. I don't know what you're talking about."

"You can tell that to the cops."

Brock struggled up from his seat and leaned over the desk, looming over Avery like a falling tree. "Do you think I'm going to lie down and play dead? All this is what I built. Look around you, Mann. Mine!"

"And you built only one S curve, just like the rest of us. Depo-Gen was your *only* claim to fame, and now you're selling out because you've run out of ideas. Unless hiring assassins to bump off your opposition is part of your new business strategy."

Brock went purple, gripping the sides of his desk like a dragon about to spew fire. But he managed to hold his tongue, survival consciousness winning over. Never react in anger was another lesson from B-school.

Avery rose. "You built an empire in the sand, if you'll pardon the pun. And you'll only understand that when the wind blows it away, like it did for me. Sand Pharmaceuticals is finished, Martin. You could take the honorable way out, walk up to the roof and jump, like Gory did. But I know you. Your kind is like the cockroach that will survive no matter what, that will find a way to wriggle out of this pickle and emerge somewhere else in a few years from now, running another shady operation. And you'll be on the phone to your spin doctors the moment I leave this room. Goodbye, Martin. Best of luck in your next iteration."

As he turned to walk out, Avery saw Brock reaching for the phone.

He paused outside the mahogany doors and took a deep breath. The PA had regained her composure by now; she had on a fresh coat of makeup, because the mascara smudges had vanished. "Everything okay, Mr. Mann?"

"Yes. Everything is okay. I've just received the final instalment of my severance package, which was long overdue. Have a nice day!"

Chapter 23

When Avery pulled into his driveway, he was ready to collapse into a long sleep. It was past 3 p.m. and he had made two stops enroute from Sand. The first had been to the RCMP office in Etobicoke, where they had difficulty understanding his mission—the Mounties were used to getting their man, not having him come to them. "I'm a witness, not the accused," he finally said in exasperation, at which point an officer was summoned, his details taken down, and a phone call made to the detachment in Nanaimo to verify his statement; two hours had elapsed. Then he stopped off at a Tim Hortons in North York for a pre-arranged meeting with Alex Mendoza. As a bonus, Avery gave the journalist Hank's letter to Olga. A jubilant Mendoza promised to be discreet and not reveal his sources.

Getting out of the van, he saw the man in the wheelchair in the opposite garden amidst the flowers, and knew he had to put his tiredness aside a bit longer. Stan Barclay was dozing in the sun, his head turned upward as if looking forward to deliverance from this mortal coil. Avery crossed the road and sat on the grass beside the wheelchair.

"Stan?"

The stroke-ridden man's head moved almost imperceptibly, and his hand rose up off the wheelchair armrest. Stan was returning his greeting.

"We won, Stan."

The eyes opened wider.

Avery leaned closer. "We beat those bastards. Phelps is going to have to do a lot of explaining."

The hand reached down from the wheelchair, gripped his, and tightened.

"It'll make the central Canada newspapers tomorrow. I'll come over and read it to you. I hope that helps you in your recovery."

The grip tightened again. Stan had spoken.

***

Avery took a shower, fell back on the couch in his pyjamas, and was out in a flash. Suddenly the clock struck 4 p.m. and he shot upright. Paul! He'd forgotten to pick up Paul after school. And Damian was supposed to be returning home tonight, if he wasn't home already, now that his offsite must have ended prematurely. *I'm one heck of an incompetent caretaker!*

He scrambled to throw on some clothes. His cell phone rang. It was Sarah. Another person he had forgotten in all the excitement!

"Hello, you're back?"

"Yes, and I'm rushing off to get Paul. I fell asleep."

"Paul's with me. I picked him up after school again today."

"You did? But I was supposed to do that."

"When I didn't hear back from you, I decided you had plenty on your hands. Besides, Paul and I are working on a project."

Avery shook his head. This was all getting a bit too much for him.

"Hello, Avery—you there?"

"Yes, I'm here. What project?"

"We're writing a story together. It's got some interesting characters in it. Some of them are drawn from real life. Paul's a budding writer."

"Well, I've got to pick him up and take him to his father."

"Damian is coming here for dinner. I phoned him, introduced myself, and invited him."

"You what?"

"Yes, he's looking forward to meeting me. And Sylvana's coming too."

"What!"

"I guess I'm an old pushy broad, but she agreed to come after I gave her a very 'persuasive' argument, shall we say. Don't get your hopes up, but I expect this could be the start of them getting back on track. They're both penitent with their split, and appear to be waiting for someone to give them the nudge that'll save face and bring them out of their corners."

"Your dinner party could end up in a screaming match with those two around."

"I don't think so. A lot has happened since you went away. I'm sure a lot's happened at your end too."

"Tell me about it! I'll need several scotches to tell you my side."

"In fact, I invited my family too. They huffed and puffed because it was a weekday, but they agreed in the end—Mother's cooking is always a draw. I think it's time the families met. Don't you think?"

"Yes, but—"

"And you are overdue for a talk with Brian, remember? I'm sure you'll have lots to tell him from your recent trip."

"Yes, but—this is happening too quickly. Aren't we supposed to be sleeping together first?" *Oh, shit, it wasn't supposed to come out like that.*

Instead of an outraged "What!" or an embarrassed silence, he heard a giggle. "Well, we are a bit late there, I agree. I was wondering when we could start."

"You seem to have this all figured out." *Can you organize my life too, woman? I've so missed that.* Syl and Damian getting together was long enough of a stretch, but sleeping with Sarah? A real second chance? However, stranger things had happened in the last twenty-four hours. Why not keep hoping and dreaming a bit longer? Hope didn't cost anything, neither did dreams.

Sarah's voice brought him out of his reverie. "Now, before we do the sleeping bit, Avery, do *you* want to come to dinner?"

Avery collapsed on the sofa laughing. "You bet I do. Are your steaks well done?"

"Yes, if you want them like that. After seeing you order steak in restaurants, much to the chagrin of the cooks, I'm going to burn yours to a crisp."

"I'm on my way."

Biography—Shane Joseph

Shane Joseph is a graduate of the Humber School for Writers in Toronto and studied under the mentorship of Giller Prize and Canadian Governor General's Award-winning author David Adams Richards. *Redemption in Paradise*, his first novel, was published in 2004. *Fringe Dwellers*, his first collection of short stories, was released in 2008, and is now in its second edition. Shane's second novel, *After the Flood,* a dystopian novel of hope, was released in 2009 and won the Write Canada Award for best novel in the futuristic/fantasy category. Shane's autobiographical novel, *The Ulysses Man,* was published in 2011, and is a fictional chronicle of the Burghers of Ceylon. Shane's fifth work of fiction, *Paradise Revisited,* a collection of short stories that continues to explore the immigrant experience, was short listed for the Re-Lit award in 2014. He covered his travels in Peru in a novel, *In the Shadow of the*

Conquistador, published in 2015. His last collection of short stories, *Crossing Limbo*, was released in 2017, followed by a novel set in small-town Ontario, *Milltown,* in 2019. His most recent novel was *Circles in the Spirals*, published in 2020.

Shane's fiction, non-fiction, and book reviews have appeared in literary journals such as the Book Review Literary Trust of India, The Wagon Magazine, Hill Spirits, Devour, and in anthologies all over the world. His blog at www.shanejoseph.com is widely syndicated and he has a monthly column in The Sri Lankan Anchorman newspaper.

More details on Shane's work, blog and public interviews can be found on his website at www.shanejoseph.com

CPSIA information can be obtained
at www.ICGtesting.com
Printed in the USA
BVHW061623090922
646661BV00014B/364